Kyselak Was Here

To Harry

Michael Robin

Kyselak Was Here

Scenes from a Life

Michael Robin

THE ASCOG PRESS

Copyright © Michael Robin 2003
First published in 2003 by The Ascog Press
Kirkokerry, Millhouse, Tighnabruaich
Argyll PA21 2BW

Distributed by Gazelle Book Services Limited
Hightown, White Cross Mills, South Rd, Lancaster, England LA1 4XS

British Library Cataloguing in Publication Data
A catalogue record for this book is available from the British Library

ISBN 0-9545989-1-1

Typeset by Amolibros, Milverton, Somerset
This book production has been managed by Amolibros
Printed and bound by T J International Ltd, Pdstow, Cornwall, UK

1. The Wanderer

Summer 1825

'... then the A ... and a K to finish off with. And the date, of course: 1825'

Kyselak stepped back to admire his handiwork. Not too far, though. The grassy ledge was fairly narrow and the drop steep enough. The stencil had definitely been a good idea. The letters were well formed and reasonably straight. It looked ... professional. Up here on a lonely rock-face in the middle of the Steinernes Meer it was unlikely that anyone would see it, perhaps the odd illiterate shepherd looking for a lost beast, but *he* knew it was there, his own name standing out proudly in the boulder-strewn desert.

The sun was bright, the rock warm and the bed of moss and grass inviting. He lay back, carefully putting his knapsack where it wouldn't go rolling down the slope, and making sure his rifle was in a safe place — he didn't want another accident.

After a lump of chewy black bread, a hunk of cheese and a mouthful of the refreshingly tart white wine from the last village — how sour it had seemed at first in the inn! — he let himself drift into a daydream. It had been a good day yesterday. Those two dairymaids! One blonde and one brunette, and he still didn't know which one!

If it hadn't been so cold in the hut he would surely have been fast asleep when she came down. Stretched out on the rough wooden bench, his knapsack under his head, fully clothed with only a threadbare horse-blanket for cover, he could still feel every bruise from his fall. First he had almost been smoked like a prime ham by the fumes from the open fire then, when it went out, the freezing cold started to eat into his bones. The shepherd boy on the bench across the room snored, and the animals in the pen outside scuffed and scraped against the side of the hut with a constant jangle of cow-bells. No wonder he'd still been awake!

And he could have been dead, never mind asleep.

It had been quite tough, the route up from St. Bartholomä on the Königssee. For a while he had to follow the course of the stream, either jumping or wading, through defiles formed by huge granite blocks and uprooted larch trunks. It was sweltering, the glare of the sun reflecting back from the banks of gneiss and mica schist. When he eventually reached the shade of the forest, the track became much steeper, so that things were no easier. At least the trees had been daubed with pitch here and there to show the way, which continued for perhaps half an hour over hollow-sounding roots, until the trunks become lower and more thickly bearded with moss, before stopping completely.

The alpine meadow was as steep and smooth as an icy roof, and the young men cutting the short grass were wearing irons on their boots. He sat down in the shade of their hut to watch them while he got his breath back. One of the women — they were singing a tune as natural as bird-song while they raked the hay — came across and told him to move out of the shade or he would get a headache and dizziness. Kyselak complied with a grateful smile, even though it was nothing more than a piece of peasant superstition.

When he asked, they couldn't tell him where the mountain cave, the so-called wind cavern, was that had been discovered less than ten years ago. Kyselak had heard about it from a huntsman in Berchtesgaden, and the description had been so cryptic and bizarre he was determined to see it for himself. A local farmer had come across it when prospecting for gold. He had not found gold but instead (exactly how was not explained) caught a fish and recovered from the jaundice that had been plaguing him for months.

He set off up the mountain and, after an hour and a half of climbing, reached the rocky labyrinth he had been told about. He found the immense limestone overhang, where the pious mountain folk had hung a wooden image of the Saviour, and saw the sugar loaves, pulpits and praying monks a lively imagination could easily form out of the jumble of boulders, but could see nothing to lead him to the cavern.

He had not spent long scrambling round among the rocks and crags, however, when four lads appeared carrying huge bundles of kindling wood wrapped up in sheets on their heads and steadying themselves with long, iron-tipped staffs.

He asked them if they knew the way to the echo cave and one immediately left his load for the others to share out among them, took up his staff and set off at such a speed Kyselak could hardly keep up with him. After half an hour they came into a gully full of limestone scree, which at least meant an end to the exhausting leaping from boulder to boulder. It was a steep climb now and they had to use hands as well as feet so as not to tumble back down onto the jagged rocks grinning up like sharp teeth below them.

Then the guide turned off between two boulders and disappeared into an opening. Kyselak was about to follow when he called back for him to bring a light and his rifle. The cave must have had a drop of some ten feet over a length of forty paces and when the guide suddenly spoke, Kyselak started at an unpleasant hissing and roaring noise that immediately filled the cavern. Every word echoed back dully from all directions and the air was so terrifyingly evil-smelling he thought he was going to suffocate.

'Fire a shot,' said the guide. 'Go on, fire a shot. There's nothing to be afraid of.'

There was a loud report and Kyselak staggered back against the wet rock, breaking out in a cold sweat which trickled down his spine. The candles went out and it seemed as if the whole cave were imploding. It was filled with flashes and flames. Kyselak could feel the rock shake with a thunder louder than cannon.

Even his guide must have felt uncomfortable. His exclamation, 'That was a bit much!' did not exactly suggest he had enjoyed the demonstration. Later he admitted he had only heard people talk of the splendid effect of a shot in the cavern and that he had no desire to repeat the experience.

They gradually recovered but — how clever of him! — he had brought the candles as instructed, but nothing to relight them with. They were plunged in darkness so deep, so black, that every step risked life and limb, especially since the cleft leading to the entrance was curved like a crescent moon, blocking out all daylight. Finally they tied their handkerchiefs and neckerchiefs together to make a guide-rope for one to lead the other. To avoid falling flat on his face on the rough ground, the guide went down on his hands and knees and crawled towards the entrance. He tied the cloth round his ankle and Kyselak held on to it. They got out into the daylight without accident, apart from a slight wetting.

Kyselak handed him a few kreuzers in payment and they hurried on their separate ways. The guide set off, unburdened, down into the valley, while Kyselak, after reloading his rifle, made his way past the cliff with the crucifix, through an immense cleft in the rocks, caused by an earthquake, and up the steep path.

Each new slope in the northward climb towards the Fundertauern was adorned with the most beautiful subalpine plants. He passed a few small huts for storing hay, but even they and all other signs of human activity had disappeared by the time he met some dairymen carrying the cheese down. Their imminent arrival was announced by large stones which came tumbling past him. Trying to escape from this rocky shower, he incautiously trod on the edge of a smooth and grassy boulder which sent him hurtling down some twenty feet. As he fell, his rifle went off, the bullet whistling over his head. Hearing cries from the descending party, he was more worried about a possible accident to them than the painful bruising to his back and legs. However, fate had resisted the temptation to stage a bloody tragedy and the men hurried down to help him.

It was usual on these scree-ridden paths, they said, to keep calling out to warn people below, and apologised for not doing so; the protruding rocks had blocked their view of anyone coming up. When the cattle were being driven up or down, they went on, it quite often happened that if the animals were not kept close together one of the beasts lower down might be injured, or frightened by the falling stones and jump to its death.

Relieved that this had not been his fate, Kyselak dragged his bruised and weary body up the last, steep climb to the Fundersee. A delightful valley surrounded by sublime peaks opened out, a green, aromatic carpet of herbs littered with bone-grey boulders. In the middle of this greenery was a hut, a romantic but ramshackle affair with crude dry-stone walls and a dilapidated roof weighted down with huge rocks; there were no windows, but plenty of gaps in the walls to let in both light and air. It looked primitive, but when the two cheerful dairymaids and the boy who herded the cows invited him to stay, he accepted with alacrity, glad to have found some shelter for the night.

Lying there in the warm sun on the grassy ledge, he savoured in his memory the simple meal he had shared with them: a somewhat lumpy porridge with slices of apple stirred in and lashings of cream poured over it. Fresh cream redolent with mountain herbs and woodsmoke, that was what it had tasted of. And that was the scent that had come to his nostrils again during the night, when a hand was suddenly placed over his mouth, his blanket lifted and someone slipped in next to him. Not a word was said, but he could feel the heat of her body through the thin shift as she pulled him close to her.

They lay entwined for a while, enjoying the warmth of the physical contact. He explored the round, firm breast and ran his hand down to her waist and along the curve of her hips, gently pulling up the shift and slipping his hand into the hotness between her thighs. His mystery partner responded, but was having difficulty with the heavy buttons of the coat he no longer needed to protect him against the cold. 'Let me …' he started to say, but again a firm hand was placed over his lips.

When she finally had the flap of his breeches open, he thrust

6

towards her to bury his throbbing member in her moist warmth, but before he could enter her, she twisted round and presented him with the ample flesh of her milkmaid's buttocks. 'Basic contraception or the standard Alpine position?' was the thought that flashed through his mind, but it disappeared unanswered as, not waiting for a second invitation, he plunged in and, after a certain amount of heaving and muffled gasping on both sides, emptied himself inside her.

He must have fallen asleep very quickly. Not very surprising really, after all he had been through since leaving St Bartholomä. The next thing he knew, he was waking up to the now-familiar smell of milk, still warm from the udder, and woodsmoke, and the sounds of the two maids going about the business of milking the cows. Some milk and toasted bread had been put out for him. When he had finished and gathered his few belongings together, he went round to the pen at the back of the hut to say goodbye and thank them for their hospitality. Without interrupting the rhythm of their hands on the teats, they looked up, smiled and wished him a safe and pleasant journey. Not by the slightest wink or flash of the eye did either indicate the hospitality had included more than simple food and a hard bench to sleep on.

Did it matter? he wondered as he set off. His friend Euler, at least, would say you didn't need to look at the tiles while you were poking the stove ...

The shepherd boy accompanied him for a while and pointed out some of the features marking the precipitous path up to the Steinernes Meer, the sea of stone. The hard overnight frost made the climb somewhat easier, although he had to keep clutching the cold clay or limestone so as not to slip with his smooth soles. As the slope eased out, he found himself humming a song he'd heard somewhere, back in Vienna probably. *On the heath a wild rose grew, / Wild rose 'mid the heather* It must have been the time — the one and only time — Hofrat Schwondrak had invited him to one of his soirées. That his boss invited him had come as a surprise, that he was not invited again less so. Perhaps he had shown too keen an interest in his daughter's décolleté while she played the piano and sang, though surely one purpose of the entertainment was to display his daughter's attractions to marriageable males, which presumably Schwondrak — or more likely his wife — had decided Kyselak was not.

And that elderly baritone, *Herr Kammer- und Hofopernsänger* Vogl, as Schwondrak had proudly announced, had certainly made sure he had a good view of the slightly daring décolleté as he sang the song 'especially for the young lady of the house'. He'd even written it himself ... no, it was his accompanist who'd written it, that rather nondescript plump chap with the receding curls and spectacles who'd spent most of the evening hidden behind the piano with a good-natured if somewhat gormless smile on his face.

It must have been the episode of the previous night that had brought the song to mind. One for the memory, definitely not for the book he was planning to write about this summer's walking tour. The censors would be quite happy with simple milkmaids trilling away in their alpine pastures, but the merest hint that he had got his oats in any other form than slightly burnt porridge would have them reaching for the red pen straight away.

As he picked his way carefully through the boulder-field, he sang out loud to the sun and the sky and a few surprised chamois.

2. *The First Time*

Summer 1817

'The first time! Do I remember the first time?!' Johann Salvator Euler's voice rang out across the small *Heuriger*. None of the guests at the other tables, immersed in their own conversations or their wine, looked up, but Euler dropped his voice to a confidential whisper — as far as anything he said could be called a whisper — as he bent forward across the table, 'It's quite a story. Did I ever tell you ...?'

Kyselak leant back. The wine, the sun on his face, the drone of Euler's voice and the music from the band in the larger wine garden across the road all induced a comfortable sense of well-being. Yes, Euler had already told him the story of what had happened when, as a fifteen-year-old schoolboy, he had gone to the little dressmaker's in the Alsergrund to collect his mother's pelisse, which had been adapted — once again — to the latest fashion. Indeed, he had heard it several times; it had gone through more changes than his mother's pelisse. It was amusing to follow its transformation — or metamorphosis, there was a good classical word! — with each successive retelling, from the fumblings of a frightened schoolboy being used by a lonely older woman (her husband had fallen during the great victory over

Napoleon at Aspern) into the brief *amour* of a debonair young Lothario who took his pleasures where he found them, this time from a 'lusty young widow, greedy for it after a long privation, if you know what I mean'.

As the *accidie* of a Viennese Sunday took hold of him, Kyselak's mind went back to his own school-days. The first time! Yes, he remembered his first time. His father was quite happy with the idea, but he had great difficulty talking his mother round. The countryside had quietened down now that the wars were over and Napoleon far away in St Helena, so it wasn't the danger that made her so unwilling to let him go off on his own on a walking tour during the summer. After all, he would soon be eighteen. In the summer he would finish school to go to university in the autumn. No, it was just that it wasn't *respectable*. To go round the countryside with a stick and a few spare clothes in a bundle, that was what wandering journeymen did, not the son of a respected if minor official of the *k.k. Patrimonial- Familien- und Avitical-Fondskasse* who was a student at the *Piaristen-Gymnasium*! He had imagined himself setting off, bundle on his back, stick in his hand, along just such a road as the one outside the *Heuriger* here in Neustift, straight out of the city into the Vienna Woods, roaming on wherever his fancy took him. But no. If he insisted on going off on an 'expedition' on foot, then he must do so out of sight of neighbours and friends.

Once his summer journey had been decided upon, his mother had thrown herself into the arrangements with her usual energy. It also provided her with an almost inexhaustible topic of conversation. 'Yes,' she said to the gossip-avid circle of cronies gathered round the coffee table, 'it'll be nice for Josef. He can visit my brother and his wife in Stein an der Donau and all the relatives in the Wachau we haven't seen for ages. His cousin Katharina in Senftenberg must be about the same age as him, perhaps a couple of years older, and they've never met. Yes, it'll be very nice for Josef to get to know my side of the family.'

And so he'd been packed off in a variety of conveyances to Melk, where he'd spent a disagreeable night in one of the monastery guest rooms. But then he'd finally been able to set out on his own, cross the Danube and follow the open road, the inviting lane, the seductive footpath until he reached Stein, where he was to take a boat back down the river to Vienna. It had been tame compared with his later journeyings, but it had been the first time he had truly been his own master and it had given him a taste for the countryside, for nature, which had since then taken him to much wilder places, to the mountains of the Tyrol and Styria, of Slovakia and Transylvania. But he still remembered that first, tame trip, that first foray out of the confines of parental protection. And he had good reason to remember it. It had signalled the start of his adult life in more than just one respect ...

'The wild rose is blooming now,
Along the hedgerows
Of the Wachau ...'

He had started singing along to the old folk tune the band opposite had struck up. Euler threw him an exasperated look. That sentimental stuff was distracting his audience. It contrasted rather awkwardly with his stories of the exploits of a ruthless male, carrying all before him, cast an ironic light on them, even.

Kyselak nodded an apology to his friend, took another mouthful of the refreshing *grüner Veltliner* and fell back into his daydreaming.

It *had* been nice to meet Cousin Katharina, very nice indeed, especially in a sleepy little village like Senftenberg. He had felt a little resentful as he knocked on the door of his aunt's house (well, his mother's sister-in-law's cousin's to be precise, the family she wanted him to get to know was extended to breaking point). The walk through the Wachau, following the course of the Danube, had only succeeded in whetting his appetite. He would really have liked to continue straight on, past Senftenberg and up the valley of the Krems, plunging into the unknown depths of the *Waldviertel* — the name conjured up in his mind pictures of virgin forest, huge trees tossing their heads in the roaring wind — and on to the heights of the Bohemian Forest, with eagles soaring above hidden lakes that lapped against precipitous cliffs … Since that first journey he had spent every summer exploring more and more remote parts of the Empire on foot. Now of course he was well acquainted with the great Bohemian Forest, that spreads its shadowy cloak over the northern edge of the little dukedom of Austria, stretching well over a hundred miles to the west, from the source of the River Thaya, just north of the pleasant valley of the Krems where he was now, to the point where the land of Bohemia meets Austria and Bavaria. That had become one of his special places, a kind of geological nodal point where, like crystals forming at the bottom of a beaker, a throng of mighty spines and ridges press against each other, thrusting up a rugged massif that displays its blue peak far and wide to the three countries, dispatching rolling hills and rushing streams in all directions. He had stood on the summit of the Plöckenstein and looked down on just such a forest-fringed lake as he was visualising while he stood there among the charming if domestic array of geraniums, paeonies and hollyhocks outside this house, the evening sun reflected in the vine-framed windows ...

'Yes? Oh, you must be Cousin Josef, I suppose. We're expecting you. We got your mother's letter.'

Kyselak came to with a start and stared at the intimidating figure before him. Who could she be, this tall, severe-looking woman with the steel-rimmed spectacles and her hair in a tight bun? She looked like an archetypal schoolmistress or governess, but surely his aunt didn't keep a governess for her only daughter, who was nineteen now, his mother had told him.

'Cat got your tongue?' she asked in her rather acid voice. 'Come in, come in. I'm Katharina, by the way. Come and meet Mother, then I'll show you to your room. I got it ready for you this morning. We were expecting you somewhat earlier.'

Confused, Kyselak mumbled an excuse in which his intended 'enjoying the beautiful local scenery' became 'enjoying the local beauties' and drew a surprising amused glance from his cousin. He just had time to present his compliments to the old lady in the frilly cap (mother? she looked more like a model grandmother, just the way he imagined kindly old Frau Holle in the fairy tale) before he was swept upstairs to a tiny room under the eaves. It was tiny but charming, with a vase of wild roses on the bedside table and a view of the ruined castle, its tower standing tall on a rocky bluff above the valley, glowing red in the rays of the setting sun.

Supper was not the inquisitorial torment he had come to fear from visits to his mother's other relatives. His aunt did quiz him a little about the doings of various members of the Vienna branch of the family, but she seemed to prefer to ramble on herself about this or that nephew and niece, brother and uncle.

The food, if simple, was satisfyingly plentiful. The table was covered with a rich variety of smoked meats and sausages — 'from my brother Albrecht in Krems, he always remembers us whenever he slaughters a beast and sends us a ham or a nice blood sausage. Things haven't been that easy for us since my poor husband was taken from us … Still, Albrecht makes sure we don't go hungry. It's quite an event when they slaughter a pig, a real party. The last time he invited Katharina to go and stay overnight … .' An image of his prim, schoolma'amish cousin dancing round the split-open carcase waving a black pudding, her tightly buttoned-up dress spattered with blood, crept irresistibly into his mind. To chase it away, he had to concentrate on his food again, and attacked a pungent goat's cheese — 'from my cousin Ferdinand who keeps goats up the valley in Reichau, well, I say cousin, but he's not really, he was the best friend of my late husband, God rest his soul, they went to school together and they used to love to go hunting together, many's the time they'd come back, frozen but with a nice deer for me to joint and cure …' Kyselak almost choked on his bread. Was that a wink Katharina had just given him? It couldn't have been. He threw a shy glance to where she was sitting, enthroned at the head of the table, ramrod straight, her angular features composed in their customary severe expression. It must have been the candles flickering on the lenses of her spectacles. He took a deep draught of wine to soothe his throat. Or perhaps he had drunk too much of the local *grüner Veltliner*? He was feeling slightly muzzy in the head already and he didn't want to make a fool of himself. Somehow his glass always seemed to be full.

'Now you two youngsters don't mind me,' said his aunt once the maid had cleared away the dishes. 'I'll just sit down in my chair and do a bit of my needlework — I'm embroidering a picture of my late husband's grave, with his dates and everything. I'll probably nod off at some point,' she added with a giggle, 'but you two just go ahead and enjoy yourselves.'

Enjoy ourselves?! What was Katharina going to propose, he wondered as she led him over to the table in the window embrasure behind her mother's wing-back armchair, a cut-throat game of Old Maid?

'I'm sure you'd like to see my flower albums,' she said in the tone of a question demanding the answer yes, 'I've got a rather interesting collection of medicinal herbs.'

She placed two thick volumes on the table in front of him. They were rather prettily bound in beige cloth with a light-blue vertical stripe interspersed with thinner stripes with elongated lozenges between them. Stamped on the front in gold was 'Katharina Oberparleiter: Garden and Wild Flowers'. The other volume simply said 'Herbs'. As she opened it, it gave off a rich, pungent, slightly musty smell.

'I collected some of these when we went to Meran last summer, but you'd be surprised what you can find just in a little place like Senftenberg. Even you will know this one. It's the common daisy. But what not many people know is that a decoction of the fresh root is excellent against the scurvy. The local peasants boil it in milk and give it to puppies to stop them growing. It doesn't work, of course, nothing will stop young puppies from growing —'

Still somewhat fuddled from the wine, Kyselak stared at the limp, shrivelled plants, all the life-giving sap dried out of them.

'— and this is valerian, you may have seen it, it has a calming, soporific effect —'

He could believe it. Just looking at it and listening to her holding forth in pedagogic tones was sending him to sleep. Katharina stretched over to turn the page

' — the gentian, the main stomachic, though people also call it the thunder plant, storms will come if you are rash enough to pick it, they say —'

and it was some time before he realised that the pressure on his arm came from her firm breast. He shifted in embarrassment, but his embarrassment turned to alarm when she rested her hand on his thigh as she pointed out a particularly fine specimen of lady's bedstraw on the page farthest away from her,

'— will cure the most violent bleedings at the nose and almost all other evacuations of blood. In the Sudetenland women put it in their beds to make childbirth easier —'

He tried to move unobtrusively to the side but found himself hemmed in by the solid table leg. She couldn't realise what she was doing, but she was setting off a reaction inside his breeches which it would be difficult to conceal if she didn't remove her hand. He sighed with relief when the gentle pressure on his thigh was released,

'— and the houseleek you'll see everywhere here because the people believe it protects their houses from storm and lightning —'

but then gasped as it returned, only this time there!, precisely on the bulge that was starting to distend his breeches. He could hardly believe it! He gave her a quick sidelong glance, but her eyes were firmly fixed on her album as she proceeded with her lecture.

16

'— eyebright is sometimes said to cure dimness of sight, but that is uncertain, to say the least —'

She clearly *did* know what she was doing as he felt her fingers through the material of his breeches squeezing and slackening, squeezing and slackening. In panic, he glanced over his shoulder and his heart missed a beat as he saw his aunt's head jerk up. Had she heard, had she seen? But then he relaxed as her head nodded back down onto her chest to the accompaniment of a quiet, bubbling snore. And still Katharina calmly continued her lecture.

' — an odd, stiff, sticky, annual species more at home in the warmer countries of the Mediterranean —'

He was beginning to enjoy the experience, when all at once his left hand was firmly grasped and placed between her legs. While he was peeping at the old woman she must have pulled up her dress! His hand was resting on soft, silky skin, warm to the touch. He felt paralysed. Despite his desire to find out the hidden secrets of the female anatomy, he didn't dare move his hand. He sat there, staring straight ahead as Katharina continued, apparently unmoved, to praise the invigorating virtues of the wild orchid

'— it is supposed to be, as the herbal puts it, a strengthener of the parts of generation and a promoter of venereal desires —'

He recovered his composure a little and decided to embark on a little furtive exploration when his whole body froze in shock: with a few deft movements she had opened the flap of his breeches. He was naked! Exposed! There! Even if concealed between the table and the wall. As she grasped him, she shifted forward, clamping his hand between her thighs. He felt with surprise the roughness of hair on the side of his hand and a wetness as his fingers were forced against soft flesh. Then all awareness of anything outside himself vanished. His insides seemed to liquidise and drop as he spilled his seed over the polished floor.

Katharina did interrupt her lecture as she squeezed his hand tight for a few seconds, before releasing him. He sat there in a daze, breathing heavily, only to be startled out of it by his aunt's voice asking, 'What are you doing down there, dear? Is anything wrong?' Hastily he fastened the flap of his breeches as he heard his cousin say, 'No, Mother, it's all right. I'm just clearing up the specimens Josef dropped on the floor.'

When she stood up, tucking a handkerchief into her sleeve, she said, without looking a him, 'Josef's tired, Mother, after all the exertion and excitement. He's going up to bed now. He wants to get up at crack of dawn tomorrow so as not to miss the best of the day for the next stage of his expedition.'

'That's very sensible,' his aunt said, nodding to him in approval. 'I don't suppose you noticed, but I dropped off for a while. I think I'll add a few more stitches to my late husband's gravestone, he'd have been proud of it, he always liked granite, he used to say ... but here's me rambling on again and you can hardly keep your eyes open. Off you go and have a good night's sleep — a clear conscience makes a soft pillow as my late husband, God rest his soul, always used to say — we'll see you in the morning.'

Kyselak leant back and stared at the roses growing in profusion against the opposite wall of the wine garden. Euler was still droning on about his conquests among the ranks of the seamstresses. Ever since what he wittily (or so he obviously thought) called his 'seminal experience' with his mother's

18

dressmaker, he had made the districts beyond the glacis of the city fortifications what he liked to call (in sentimental rather than witty mode this time) the 'hunting grounds of his heart'. These largely lower-middle-class districts were full of small workshops, carpenters, glaziers, wheelwrights, potters, tailors and, of course, dressmakers. And employed there was many a young girl who was willing to grant her favours to a 'gentleman' who could afford to give her the 'good time' that was likely to be all too rare in her subsequent marriage. Nice girls, some of them, pretty too, though not really Kyselak's cup of tea ...

Suddenly his memory was tweaked by the smell of coffee being carried past for the women at the next table. Coffee ... and roses ...

He had woken up the next morning in his aunt's house to the smell of coffee, the appetising smell of coffee, even if in 1817, when the country was still exhausted from the wars and the expenses of the Congress, the main ingredient was chicory. Dawn had clearly already cracked in this household, so he washed and dressed quickly, then hurried down, but paused outside the dining-room, unsure how to behave towards Katharina. He pushed the door open to be greeted by her habitual schoolma'amy look. Abashed, he slunk over to the table, muttering an excuse for what he presumed they would think of as his late rising. She came over and placed a bowl of coffee in front of him with a glance that showed a slight softening of the severe features, even the hint of a wink. As she took her hand away from his bowl, the back, as if by chance, gently stroked his cheek. For a second she stood still, as if in a dream then, jerking back into her everyday persona, said to his aunt, 'Mother, Josef wants to go and have a look at the castle before he heads off down to Krems,' and swept out of the room.

'Oh yes, the castle, you really must see that. The Baron has put a lot of work into restoring it, or at least stopping it from falling down any more. He doesn't live there himself, you know, it's a ruin really, his house is farther up the valley, you should see that too, it's covered all over with roses and just now they're in full bloom … lovely … we have some in our little garden, my late husband — how he loved his garden — he planted them, but there's no comparison, at the big house they're all colours, from white and yellow to the deepest crimson … Rose Hall you could call it … and the Baron's very keen on preserving and restoring all the local antiquities, very learned he is about that kind of thing, only just now, because of the difficult times, he's had to call a temporary halt, but the scaffolding's still there, so you'll be able to have a clamber around, if you want, I'm sure a healthy young lad like yourself loves climbing and scrambling over rocks and ruins. As my late husband used to say …'

Kyselak sang as he set off on as beautiful a summer's morning as a man could wish for:

The wild rose is blooming now
Along the hedgerows
Of the Wachau.
A cottage peeps through the vines,
There lives a girl,
I know she'll be mine …

The castle was little more than a tower rising up from a steep rock above the village. It did indeed have scaffolding round it

20

and Kyselak climbed up and looked at the panorama of rolling hills disappearing into a blue haze. The glorious view, the balmy air, the bird-song, the unaccustomed freedom of the last four weeks and, above all, the experience of the previous evening caused an outpouring of vague but exhilarating emotion. He ached to do something — anything — to give it concrete expression. An abandoned pot of creosote, the brush still sticking in it, caught his eye. He grabbed it and started to daub his initials and those of Katharina surrounded by a heart on a barrier of rough wooden planks blocking off the drop into the empty courtyard. But he stopped and painted it over, blotting it out with savage, stabbing brushstrokes. It seemed too trite, too much of a cliché for the emotions seething inside him (and someone might recognise her initials and embarrass her with questions about her secret admirer). He felt he had come of age, he was a man, an individual who had something to say for himself. He looked up at the wall above him and, on a sudden inspiration, climbed to the top level of the scaffolding and scrambled up the crumbling side of a window embrasure where the stones stuck out like steps. Standing erect on the very top, he threw his arms wide in a gesture as if to embrace the whole world and its millions. Then, carefully leaning over the side, he wrote his name in large black letters for all to see: KYSELAK, 1817, as if to say *veni, vidi, vici*, Kyselak was here.

3. The Anninger Hermit

Summer/ Autumn/ Winter 1819

'The Grace of the Immaculate Conception, which we celebrate in Maria today, is not a simple, but a multifold Grace, encompassing within it several of God's Graces. Through our Conception, we miserable men and women have inherited from our forefather Adam, and brought with us into this world, not only Original Sin, but also Lust, which is a punishment of Original Sin. In my sermon today I intend to demonstrate I: the Nature of Lust; II: how the Devil uses Lust to ensnare us, and III: how we can conquer Lust.'

'Why on earth did I let myself be dragged along here?' Kyselak groaned to himself as Imperial Royal *Hofprediger* Johann Nepomuk Tschuppik set off on Section I, Subsection 1, Part a) of the theme of his sermon that he was evidently going to pursue doggedly through its 'multifold' twists and turns all the way to Section III, Subsection 3, Part c).

He threw a covert glance at his old school friend, who had persuaded him to come and hear the celebrated chaplain-in-ordinary to the imperial court. Franz Karl was sitting, hands clasped, eyes fixed on the handsome, if somewhat saturnine figure in the pulpit, in an attitude of eager and devout expectation. His clothes had a semi-clerical cut, suggesting the candidate for the priesthood he would soon become.

They had known each other at school, the *Piaristen-Gymnasium* in the Josefstadt, but since then their lives had taken different courses. Kyselak had entered the university with the idea of eventually becoming a lawyer, but Franz Karl had gone into his father's business, a small firm making glass objects — cups and vases — decorated with portraits of members of the imperial house or pretty landscapes. After only one year of that, however, he had suddenly announced his desire to go to the university to study theology as a preparation for entering the priesthood. Fortunately, there was a brother to take over the business, and a priest in the family was generally regarded as a good thing, a kind of spiritual insurance policy, though it was usually the younger offspring who were determined for that role.

He had met Franz Karl again some eight months ago as the latter was coming out of the Church of the Jesuits by the University. His old school friend had been full of enthusiasm for his vocation. He invited Kyselak round to his room, where they talked long into the night about God, the Church and the need for a spiritual revival in Austria. 'The Church has become a kind of religious bureaucracy,' Franz Karl had declared, 'a prop of Metternich's system, the spiritual arm of Sedlnitzky's police, a kneeling army of priests to back up the standing army of soldiers.' — A nice image, thought Kyselak, but I'm sure someone else said it first. — 'We need a renewal of genuine belief, and people must be filled with enthusiasm for the Faith and live out their lives according to their beliefs.'

23

Dangerous talk. Everyone knew that in the Emperor's eyes any enthusiasm, even patriotism, was suspect. There was a story going the rounds of a woman telling Emperor Franz that her son had decided to give up his studies to become a priest. 'If you like,' the Emperor was said to have replied, 'I will have the matter investigated by the police.'

Kyselak shot another sidelong glance at his friend. There was no denying the intensity of his religious fervour, the force of his commitment. And yet Kyselak wondered how exclusive the vocation was. Was it completely unsullied by thoughts, perhaps unacknowledged thoughts, of advancement? There was a hint of elegance about his well-made proto-clerical suit, a fire in his dark brown eyes and a physical attractiveness about the chestnut locks falling over his forehead which suggested that given the right — or wrong — impetus he could end up as a fashionable priest with a following of well-to-do ladies. With a rather jaundiced eye, Kyselak surveyed the colourful silk dresses crammed into the front pews, elaborate hats tilted at an angle as their wearers gazed up at the tall figure of the *Hofprediger*. Were they taking in a single word of what he was saying in his slight Bohemian accent?

'This Lust we have inherited from Adam is simply the violent desire we feel for certain things. According to the teaching of Saint John the Divine, it is threefold: Concupiscentia carnis, *the Lust of the Flesh, by which Man follows his Natural Urge to seek things appealing to his Bodily Senses: pleasant food and drink, comfortable clothes, a soft bed to lie on, the satisfaction of Carnal Desire etc. Secondly,* Concupiscentia oculorum, *the Lust of the Eyes ... thirdly* Superbia vitae, *the Pride of Life ... Before his Fall into Sin, Adam was master*

over these temptations of the Human Heart, none of these Lusts could appear unless he had first given his permission ...'

Tschuppik's undoubted hold over his bevy of devotees seemed to come from externals: from his tall figure and handsome features, the almost mesmeric look in his black eyes and the flowing lines and tasteful decoration of his vestments. His voice was deep and resonant, but those rich sounds only served to cloak the paucity of feeling in the words and ideas they expressed. How different from Father Hofbauer, into whose orbit his old school friend had initially gravitated. Recently, however, he seemed to be drifting in the direction of the more mondain priesthood represented by Tschuppik.

Father Hofbauer was a different kettle of fish entirely. It was almost as if his unprepossessing appearance were deliberately designed to confuse potential disciples. His powerful, bull-necked physique suggested the butcher he had originally been, but as soon as he grew animated, he exuded an openness, a fullness of personality, a warmth which immediately enveloped the listener. No tedious traipse through the Seven Deadly Sins for him. Instead of Lust (which Tschuppik was still doggedly trying to pin down, like an entomologist a dead and dried-up butterfly) he spoke of love. And when he spoke of it, you felt that he was himself fired by it. 'Open up your hearts to God's love,' he would say, 'open up your hearts and minds to the love that is all around you, and to the love that is within you.' Of course he would go on to make a distinction between *agape* and *eros* (how useful a classical education was for finding polite words to talk about facts some might find embarrassing!). And he did not condemn lust as a sin, but emphasised the part it had to play in life as long as it was

25

kept subordinate to the greater love of God and one's fellow man. '*Eros* should be the handmaid of *agape*,' he would say. It was, perhaps, unfortunate that the phrase always brought the memory of Cousin Katharina to Kyselak's mind.

At the meetings to which Hans Karl took him, Kyselak had often found himself carried away by the impact of Hofbauer's personality and would go home resolved to lead a better life. On the other hand, after he had had a couple of glasses of wine at the *Heuriger*, he would feel ashamed of the strait-laced piety of the religious circle. He was certainly glad his drinking companions knew nothing about his attendance. He could well imagine the jokes Euler would make if he knew.

Unlike Euler, for whom *eros* was the often-proclaimed be-all and end-all of his relations with women, Kyeslak hoped he would find an ideal love that would unite sensual, intellectual and spiritual companionship. He hoped to find a woman with whom he would share his life, not just bed and board. Even if it was not quite the same thing, it helped him understand Hofbauer's *eros/agape* distinction. But the teaching still had the stale taste of dogma for him. Despite Hofbauer's emphasis on the positive, Kyselak sensed behind him the dead hand of the church. What had Hans Karl called the church during that long discussion? 'The spiritual arm of Sedlnitzky's police'? For Kyselak it was much more than that. 'Existential police' was how he thought of it. It tried to get its clutches on everyone at an early age and fill them with guilt as a means of keeping them in its power, under control.

The atmosphere in the Kyselak household had never been particularly devout. The rather dour rationalism his father had picked up from the older generation of civil servants who continued the tradition started under Emperor Josef — 'If God exists, then he'll listen to reason, and that's what I do. I've no time for incense and miracles and men in fancy dress, they only cloud the mind. I use what reason God gave me, little though it may be, and do my best to follow it.' — was not particularly attractive to him, but it did shield him against excessive submissiveness to the clergy.

Kyselak still remembered the liberating effect of his first excursion alone and his visit to Katharina. The combined effect of freedom to go where he liked and what he, in those younger days, called their 'lovemaking' had produced a euphoria that lasted until he was on the boat and watching the twin spires of Klosterneuburg Abbey appear against the backdrop of the Vienna Woods. In the deflation that naturally followed, he had wondered what to do. Should he reveal it at confession, which his mother still expected him to attend? The more he thought about it, and he spent a lot of time thinking about the experiences of those four weeks away from home, the less he could see it as a 'sin'. Despite the necessarily furtive nature of their fumblings under the heavy oak table, he could not see them as something that degraded him, that needed excusing, never mind regret and atonement. Much of this was due to the impression his cousin had made on him. She had taken him without fuss, as if it were the most natural thing in the world, he told himself. Of course, for the church 'natural' as good as meant sinful. He could just imagine the hoops Tschuppik would make the concept jump through in one of his sermons! But his encounter with the unspoilt countryside of his homeland had led him to equate 'natural' with 'good'. He kept his confession to vague, generalised admissions of the kind of things boys of his age were supposed to be troubled by: 'unclean thoughts, Father,' 'disobedience towards those in authority over me, Father,' 'pride in my own cleverness, Father.' It kept the priest happy and that kept his mother happy. But he still remembered the liberating effect of not feeling *obliged* to feel guilt. There were things he felt guilty about, yes, but he assessed them and tried to deal with them himself.

The liberation had not been so sudden and so clean as it seemed in retrospect, but it did mean that the one dogma he could not accept was the doctrine of original sin. There was evil in people, but there was also good, and for him neither predominated. From his experiences, in particular with the peasant folk out in the country, Kyselak could not believe man was innately marked by sin. Evil had been done to him, certainly: things had been stolen, once even his boat when he was on his way down the Inn, he had encountered suspicion, been deceived and turned away. But these had been the exceptions. He had met with so much kindness, so much honesty, so many who insisted on sharing their simple food with him and refused any payment, that original sin seemed to make no sense. But if you took away original sin, did you not take away the keystone that held the church's system of belief — and even more, its system of control — together?

Anyway, thought Kyselak, as Tschuppik made his tortuous way into Section III of his sermon, dull, dry doctrine did not interest him in the least. The contemplative life, though, that certainly had its attractions. There was that priest — a professor of theology or philosophy, perhaps even both? — who had been dismissed for publishing something the authorities decided they didn't like. — They were coming down very hard on students and professors alike just now since the rather stupid murder of a reactionary hack by a student. Perhaps Metternich's agents had put him up to shooting Kotzebue? — But the professor who had been dismissed had apparently been unconcerned, saying he looked forward to spending the rest of his days studying and writing in the calm of his monastery.

Kyselak sometimes visualised himself in a simple, whitewashed cell, the wintry sunshine streaming in through the high, narrow window, a large tome open in front of him on the rough deal table. Botany was his special study, and he advised those who worked on the monastery farm and in the vineyards. Especially the vineyards. There were orders that lived quite a pleasant life as far as physical comforts were concerned. He studied the vines, crossed different strains and developed a new variety of grape that made a rich, fragrant wine much appreciated by the grateful brothers. But he modestly rejected the suggestion the variety should be named 'Kyselakia'. No, he would decide, it should be named after the monastery …

Huh! With his luck he was much more likely to end up in a monastery with rigid rules, more like a prison than a community of like-minded ascetics and scholars, with petty jealousies and backbiting rife among his fellow monks. And with superiors who lived a life of elegance and luxury while the rank and file were condemned to soulless drudgery. He would run away, seek his fortune somewhere where his talents could develop, could flourish. To America, where they said every man was free to think and do and write and publish what he liked. But how would he support himself? He couldn't even speak English. And what could he do? Add up a column of figures correctly and write a clear and concise report in a neat hand. That was unlikely to get him far in the land of the free. Just a minute, though. There *was* something he could do — his carpentry and cabinet-making. Here in Austria it was not considered suitable work for anyone who belonged to the educated classes. It had to be a hobby for him, nothing more, and even then he kept it as secret as possible.

But in America? He could just see himself in the small town, a pretty place on the edge of the immense forests that covered much of the continent. A respected member of the community, respected for his skill with his hands. In the evening he would come back from his workshop to a wholesome meal cooked by his wife, work in the garden, listen to his children say their lessons, then settle down to read and write. 'A real scholar,' his neighbours would say. And they would respect him for that as well, but no more than they respected him for his solid carpentry and the sensible advice he gave at town meetings. And there would be plenty of wild spaces for him to roam with his trusty rifle. Perhaps he would still be able to go off for a week or two in the summer, fending for himself and living out in the open, doing a pioneering study of the flora and fauna of the region. He would become a well-known figure to the local Indians. They would give him a name of their own. 'Herb-Gatherer' or 'Flower-Picker', 'Pathfinder' or 'Deerslayer' or something like that.

That was a fantasy he could realise if he had the strength and the energy. All he needed to do when next summer came was to pack his knapsack, take his woodworking tools and the little money he had saved and set off across Germany to Hamburg. Work his passage as a ship's carpenter.

Hamburg, August 1820

My dearest, beloved Parents,
As you can see, I am in Hamburg. The ship sets sail this
evening. By the time you read this I will be in the middle
of the Atlantic Ocean, on my way to America …

No. Even if he could summon up the courage to cut his ties
with his homeland and set off into the unknown, he could not do
that to his parents. He knew it would remain a dream.

If he was looking for a spiritual mentor — which he wasn't — he
would much prefer the strange fellow he had met on the Anninger
hill above Gumpoldskirchen. The hermit. Or semi-hermit, as the
man had said with disarming honesty. His self-deprecating
honesty was one of the things that had attracted Kyselak to him.
He had none of the spiritual pride which so many of the capital's
clergy seemed to display — though not Hofbauer, not the
'Apostle of Vienna' as people called him. The 'Anninger hermit'
seemed to have found a mode of life which fitted him perfectly. It
wasn't a ready-made model of behaviour you could preach to
other people, and Kyselak did not feel impelled to organise his
own life in the same way. But what he found attractive, beside the
man's innate modesty and courtesy, was the way he seemed in
harmony with himself and with the world around, at least the
natural world of the Anninger.

It was not much over two months ago, just at the beginning of
October, that Kyselak had met him. He had spent the summer in
the mountains of the Tyrol, but an Indian summer had seduced
him into making one last excursion before winter set in for good.
Early one Saturday morning he had taken the *diligence* as far as

Perchtoldsdorf, then made his way through the woods to Hinterbrühl, climbed the Kleiner Anninger and walked along the ridge to the main summit. He had been very tempted by the *Husarentempel*, the memorial to the Austrian soldiers who had fallen in the war against Napoleon. Standing on a conspicuous spur of the hill above Mödling, the Greek temple designed by Kornhäusel, resplendent in white and yellow paint, simply cried out for him to write 'KYSELAK, 1819' on it. But somehow he felt to do so would have desecrated the memory of the soldiers who had given their lives for their emperor, and so for once he resisted the temptation to leave his signature.

Though autumn had arrived, it was pleasantly mild and he was prepared to have to spend the night out in the open. However, he was delighted to come across a cave in the side of a shallow gully running down from the summit. It was below a large pine which must have been stunted at some point in its life, as its gnarled and twisted branches spread out wide instead of thrusting up into the sky. In fact it was his curiosity about the unusually shaped tree which led to the discovery of the cave. It had an oddly cared-for look. The dead leaves seemed to have been swept up and the floor was clear of loose stones and gravel. At the back was a simple cross made of two branches bound together with a leather thong. Someone must use it as a kind of chapel, but Kyselak was sure they would not mind a weary wanderer seeking shelter for the night there. Not that he needed shelter yet, the evening was dry and still warm. He sat on his old blanket in the mouth of the cave, observing the woods outside as twilight thickened into night.

It was still. The only noises were the scurryings of small night creatures through the twigs and across the carpet of pine needles.

Then a louder, or at least a more substantial noise started, as if some larger animal were prowling about, to and fro, round the cave, just out of sight behind the trees and bushes. Was he occupying its lair? Surely there would have been a strong scent if an animal used the cave, and the cross and cleanly swept floor suggested humans visited it regularly. In the Carpathians he might be afraid he was keeping a bear from its shelter, but not in the Vienna Woods. The noise continued, a strange scuffling and shuffling. Perhaps a badger was out hunting, though it was a bit high up for one of them. If he believed in spirits, he might imagine the ghost of the Anninger had come to haunt him.

He had heard about the ghost when Euler and the rest of them had hired a char-à-banc to come out to a *Heuriger* in Gumpoldskirchen. Euler was very partial to the rich, golden *Gumpoldskirchner*. They had got talking to the grower whose wine they were enjoying, and he told them the story, which he had, so he claimed, from the neighbour of the brother of the man who had seen the ghost. 'Almost as good as from the horse's mouth itself.'

Sepp Perchtinger had been to a wedding in Hinterbrühl and had decided, the night being fine, to make his way back over the hill. However, despite the fact that there was a full moon, he became confused as to the way — perhaps not unconnected with the fact that the groom was a fellow wine-grower — and when he found a cave he decided to rest there and wait until it got light. He stretched out in the mouth of the cave and dropped off to sleep. After some time, how long he couldn't tell, he awoke with a start. Whatever his state before, he was now stone-cold sober. He didn't know if some sound had woken him, but he felt cold, colder than he would have expected, given that it was a fine night in midsummer. It was as if he were enveloped in a cocoon of chilly air. There was still no noise, but there was a smell. A sweet, sickly smell, the smell of rotting flesh. He looked up to check how far round the moon had got, and there he saw the figure of a man. It was swinging to and fro on a rope from a branch of the crooked pine tree above the cave. Its eyes were bulging and looking straight at him. One arm stretched out ...

Sepp leapt up and ran as fast as he could, anywhere as long as it was downhill. He didn't stop until he came out of the woods onto the open and familiar slope of a vineyard, where he lay down and slept until the sun rose and he could see the spire of Gumpoldskirchen church only a mile away to the north.

The apparition Sepp had seen was the ghost of Fraunwallner, the hermit of the Anninger. He had supposedly lived in the cave some forty years previously. What had made him become a hermit, no one knew. And no one had the opportunity to find out, because he carefully avoided all contact with the local population. With one exception, that is. From time to time he obviously felt the need for contact — intimate contact — with a woman. It was usually an unfortunate farm girl or maidservant he fell upon as they went home from a fair or a dance. When he had finished with them, he disappeared into the darkness, though not without leaving a gift, a carved wooden spoon, the handle decorated with foliage.

It was this that had eventually given him away. To make some money for food, he sold his carved spoons to a shopkeeper in Vienna and a wine merchant from the city had recognised the workmanship when, on a visit to buy wine, he had been told about the local rapist who gave his victims presents. Fraunwallner was captured by the police when he next went to Vienna to sell his wares, and was put in prison. He hated it. He pined for the solitude and freedom of the Anninger. And he escaped, helped, it was said, by a woman. Foolishly, he went back to the Anninger, where he was soon surrounded by the police and troops. Rather than be taken and locked up again, he hanged himself from the crooked pine above his cave.

It was a story Kyselak had enjoyed, but did not believe. 'If there are ghosts and they're spirits, they're not going to be able to do me any physical harm,' his father used to say, 'and that's all I'm afraid of.' The strange scuffling had stopped. It was quiet again, except for the creaking of the tree as the wind got up. But the wind had not got up, it was still as calm as it had been all day. He looked out and started in surprise as he saw, on the ground outside the cave, the shadow of a tall man swinging to and fro from a branch of the pine, one arm stretched out. And there was a smell. A strong smell, certainly, but not a sickly one. That was definitely the odour of a living human being, if a very unwashed one. He looked up at the figure hanging from the tree, protuberant eyes staring at him.

'You'd better come down now,' he said, 'your arm must be getting tired.'

The figure stared at him with its wide, bulging eyes, said, 'Aha, not an ignorant local, then,' dropped to the ground and came down the slope to the cave.

Kyselak stood up. 'Josef Kyselak,' he said with a slight bow. 'I'm sorry if I've taken your cave, but I assumed it was uninhabited, since there's nothing in it but the cross. I like to go walking in the hills and mountains by myself and often spend the night out of doors. The cave seemed a good spot.'

'I see,' said the other. 'The cave is empty because I keep my things hidden in a cleft behind that bush over there, ever since I had my little store of food and my blanket and knife stolen.' He thought for a moment. 'Is that Kyselak spelt K-y-s-e-l-a-k, by the way? Are you the one who wrote his name in large letters on the Rauhenstein ruin above Baden, then? How you got up there to do it, I can't imagine. Risking your neck just to shout out to all the elegant *Kurgäste* strolling up the Helenental, "I've been here!" The things you young people get up to nowadays.'

The elongated shadow cast by the moon had turned into a short, stocky man with a bushy white beard. He was wearing a wide-brimmed, grey felt hat that was almost conical, and a long, shapeless garment that had echoes of a monk's habit. His bare feet were in what looked like home-made sandals. Standing in the shadow of the pine tree, he looked like a giant boletus mushroom.

'So it was you who were prowling round in the shadows?'

'Yes, I'm afraid it was. You see, I'm a hermit. Well, semi-hermit would be more precise. It's not that I absolutely refuse to talk to other people, but I do like to keep myself to myself. And the locals can be a bit of a nuisance. They regard me as an eccentric and sometimes used to come to watch me. Like a street juggler. There was a time when those of them who make a living from the summer visitors regarded me as a local attraction and used to send their guests along to view the 'genuine Anninger hermit'. I do prefer to avoid them if I can. Hans Haimon, by the way.'

'Does living in a place that is supposed to be haunted attract them even more, or frighten them off, Herr Haimon?'

'Ah.' A glint came into his slightly protuberant eyes. 'So you've heard the story?'

'Yes. One of the wine-growers in Gumpoldskirchen told us. He said a neighbour of his had seen it, I think.'

'He did, did he? Well in that case it must be true. In general it keeps the locals well away, especially at night. The visitors from Vienna are another matter. There was one who declared he wasn't afraid of ghosts and obviously wanted to be able to boast of having spent the night in a 'haunted cave' when he went back to the city. My little performance was more effective on him than on you, though the stage effects were better. A storm was rising and there was a fitful moon, just the night for a ghost.'

'So you use the story to keep unwelcome visitors away?'

'Well, to tell you the absolute truth,' the mischievous glint reappeared in his eye and he grinned, 'I invented the story myself, though it has been elaborated a bit since I first told it. I've no idea who this Sepp Perchtinger is! One evening I went down to a wine-garden in Gumpoldskirchen — in everyday clothes, not in my hermit's garb — and got talking to a group of local farmers. When we were on to the fifth or sixth glass, I told them of the horrible experience I had had when I was lost in the woods one night. "That must be the ghost of Fraunwallner," one of them said. "He hung himself from the crooked pine." I pretended I had never heard of Fraunwallner. A few days later a couple of young boys appeared, but I soon frightened them off with a bit of shuffling among the dead leaves and making branches creak ominously. I didn't even have to do my hanging-from-the-branch routine.'

'If you live as a hermit, I can understand you not wanting to be disturbed by other people, especially ones who look on you as a kind of fairground attraction. I can respect that. I'll go and find another spot to spend the night. It's dry and warm, I don't need shelter, my blanket'll do.'

'No, no. Stay. I can see you are a kindred spirit, in some ways, if you like being alone in nature. You live in the capital?'

'Yes, but I spend every summer walking in the mountains.' (Only two summers so far since that first expedition, if he were honest, but the intention was there and that was what counted.) 'This year I was in the Tyrol. — I have plenty of cheese and fresh bread in my knapsack, by the way, if you would care to share it?'

'Delighted. I may live out in the wilds, and I'm happy to make do with whatever food I happen to have, but I don't believe in mortifying the flesh unnecessarily. The bread I have is a week old and the sausage to go with it, though very tasty, is rather dry. But the water is delicious. It comes from a well lower down the hill. I was bringing some back when I saw you.'

The hermit went to the hidden cleft and brought out his blanket, a knife, a jug of water and two plain but neatly made pottery tumblers. ('Two because I'm somewhat clumsy and liable to drop my cup or knock it over.') Both set about the bread, cheese and sausage with a healthy appetite.

'Do you live here all the year round?' asked Kyselak.

'No. Only during the summer. That's why I called myself a 'semi-hermit'. 'Fair-weather hermit' might be nearer the mark, I suppose. I'm not usually here this late. I'll be off back to Vienna as soon as this beautiful spell breaks. I've been coming here every summer for ten years now. I started like you, wandering by myself and spending more and more nights out in the open, though' — he patted his comfortable paunch — 'I stuck to the hills and

38

valleys, the mountains are not for me. I found this place by chance and gradually made it my permanent summer home.'

'How do you spend your winters, if you don't mind my asking?'

'In Vienna. I have a good position there, though you might not think it from my present dress — and my present smell. There is a pool where I bathe, but I only do it once a week, generally on Mondays. You get used to your own smell, however strong it is. That says a lot about being a hermit, I think. — As I was saying, I have a good position. I work as confidential clerk for a merchant who imports a variety of goods, anything from raisins to skins, silks and porcelain. His business is almost entirely with the southern countries, Italy, Greece, the Levant, so he does most of his travelling there in the winter, to avoid the summer heat. He trusts me absolutely. He knows I won't cheat him or neglect the business while he's away and so he lets me take the summer off, which he spends in Vienna anyway.

'I have a very pleasant apartment just behind St. Stephen's. As I said, being a hermit doesn't mean I have any objection, moral or otherwise, to creature comforts, it's just that I refuse to let my life be dominated by them. I can enjoy a jug of new wine as much as the next man, but I am also quite happy to live on the water from the Martinsbründl at the bottom of the slope for weeks if necessary.'

Suiting action to word, he took a drink from his mug, then went on, 'I don't actively avoid people in the capital, but as I have no relatives, no colleagues or circle of friends, there is no one I come into close contact with. The clerical work for the business is done by a man who had an accident and is housebound. His daughter comes twice a week to collect the material and bring back the completed work.' For a while he said nothing, but just hummed quietly to himself. He suddenly stopped and looked at Kyselak, as if he had forgotten he was there.

'My greatest joy is music. I go to concerts whenever I can. I even go to church, but I have to admit it is only for the music. I'm afraid all the rest seems like mumbo-jumbo to me, but there will be others for whom it is meaningful, I am sure. I play myself, the violin. With a certain degree of proficiency, I think I may say. Sometimes I play simple folk tunes, then improvise on them. Fantasise might be a better word. I can go on for hours. I delight in the sounds themselves, and in the way they combine in melody, in richer and richer harmonies, then dissolve into discord, to come together again, gradually, tentatively, like the hands of shy young lovers.' Herr Haimon paused for a moment and stared at the stars. It was almost as if he had been musing to himself.

'I also play compositions. Some by an old master called Bach are particularly dear to me. A single line of his music can seem to weave and interweave, can seem to be two or three voices at once. I feel as if I am on a higher plane when I play them, as if things were being revealed to me that I am unaware of in my ordinary existence — and that I have forgotten when the music ends, though I am left with the memory of a greater harmony.' He closed his rather bulging eyes and nodded meditatively.

'I sometimes think, Herr Kyselak, that listening to music must be the same for me as going to church for other people. To hear, say, the second movement of Haydn's string quartet in D major, opus seventy-six, number five,' — he quoted the full title, seeming to roll it appreciatively round his tongue, like a fine wine — 'to be immersed in the music, is like contemplating the order of the universe, music of the spheres. To play it with three like-minded partners must be an intense joy, must be what those of a religious disposition imagine heaven is like — if they are capable of imagining it.

'One regret of my solitary existence is not to have such a group of friends with whom I can play the masterpieces of Haydn, Mozart or Beethoven. Still, one must learn to be content with what one has. I think that if I went out to look for fellow musicians to play with I would be likely to lose as much as I would gain.'

He leant back, looking up at the stars again. Hesitantly, Kyselak asked, 'Do not answer this if it seems intrusive, but are there other regrets you have for the way of life you have chosen?'

Haimon thought for a while. 'I am quite happy to tell you. I would hate to mislead you into thinking the solitary life offers perfect fulfilment. Sometimes I sit on a rocky bluff lower down with an open outlook and watch people walking along the path to Baden. It is a favourite walk of Beethoven's. It always puzzles me how a man who looks so out of sorts with himself and the world can write such sublime music. I'm sure Haydn didn't go round with a permanent scowl on his face. With Haydn, you know, I sense the glory of the world as it is, with Beethoven an intimation of what the world could be like, *should* be like, maybe … But there I go, rambling on about my music again. What I wanted to say was that when I look down and see the families out for a walk together — father, mother, sons and daughters — I feel a strong regret that it has not been my lot to be surrounded by children. The joy of watching them growing up, developing, looking for new experiences, discovering the world. There was a girl …'

Herr Haimon paused and was silent for a while. Soon a contented, rumbling snore indicated that he had fallen asleep.

Kyselak pulled his blanket round him, lay back and stared at the sky, the stars only faintly visible in the light of the full moon.

Life as a hermit, as a 'semi-hermit' even? No, that was not what he wanted, even though there was something attractive about the way Herr Haimon seemed in harmony with himself. But how had he achieved it? 'There was a girl …' Haimon's last words suggested it was less the fruit of fulfilment than of renunciation. An old man's contentment with what he had. Despite the similarity in the way they spent their summers, Kyselak had no intention of abandoning the hope of achieving something, of making something of his life.

What did he want to do? What did he want to be? Certainly not the head of a happy family leading his wife and children along the pleasant footpaths of the Prater or the Helenental on sunny Sunday afternoons.

He sometimes saw himself as the Wanderer, a brooding, romantic figure making his lonely way over cliffs and crags, through primeval forests, past raging torrents, exulting in the violence of the thunderstorm, pouring his experiences of wild nature into impassioned song.

He knew that this was a fanciful image, that he cut a less than romantic figure when he arrived at some mountain hut, soaked to the skin, covered in mud and rather hungry. Yet his summers spent walking in the mountains were important to him, to the real Kyselak, they were not just a role he played out. He needed them. Without them he felt the rest of the year would be almost unbearable. And he felt they fed into his poetry, even when he was not writing about the things he saw and experienced on his solitary wanderings. They seemed to fill him with a kind of spiritual energy he did not find in church.

If he intended to continue to live a split life like Herr Haimon, three summer months in the mountains, the rest of the year in Vienna, then he would have to renounce some things. A house and home with wife and children — which he did not want, anyway — hardly fitted in with that.

But did that mean he would have to renounce love? Not lust. He was still too timid or too afraid — afraid of being robbed, afraid of some awful disease — to imitate his friend Euler and follow the countless invitations on the darker street-corners and alleys of Vienna. But during his excursions in the country he had several times been given more than a roof over his head and a bite to eat. He was surprised at the number of girls and women, cooks and dairymaids, a country carpenter's widow, a blacksmith's daughter, who had seen in this passing stranger the opportunity for sensual pleasure, and had seized it. They enjoyed themselves with him as if it were the most natural thing in the world, and happily parted the next day. Well, he had once spent a whole week with the carpenter's widow, playing the part of journeyman carpenter in the workshop during the day and dovetailing with the widow at night. His hobby of cabinet-making had come in useful there!

But love? Was that just another romantic illusion, like the figure of the Wanderer, or was it something more deeply rooted within him? After his experience in the Tyrol that summer he suspected it was the latter …

It had been among the soaring peaks of the Zillertal. It was also in the pouring rain of the Zillertal and he was soaked through. He had taken refuge in a cowshed, where he had been found, crouched between two of the beasts for warmth, by the daughter of the house as she came to milk the cows. She was a tall, well-built girl, handsome rather than beautiful. He explained his predicament and asked if he might spend the night there, to dry out and get warm. She gave him a long look of appraisal, then told him to wait while she did the milking, then she would 'come and see to him'.

When she returned she didn't tell him to fill an empty stall with straw, as he had expected, or at least hoped. She took him by the hand and led him round the back of the stable and into a narrow stand of fir trees above the farmhouse. Behind them was a small but neat and cosy-looking cottage, single-storied with an attic window.

'It's the *Ausgedinge*,' she explained. 'My grandparents moved in here when they handed over the farm to my father. My grandmother died last year. It's been empty since then and will be until my father decides he's had enough, but it's looked after. It's clean and dry, you'll be more comfortable there than in the byre.'

She took him inside and placed a bundle of food she'd brought in her apron — an apple, some sausage, a few pieces of sweet pancake — on the table.

'You'll have to be quiet,' she said, 'my father's very suspicious of strangers. He thinks everyone from the city is a thief. No candles, and you won't be able to light a fire, of course, but if you hang your wet clothes up on the line in the loft, they should dry out quite well. I can see you're soaked to the skin. There's some blankets in that cupboard, so I suggest you get the whole lot off and wrap yourself up well. I've got to go now or they'll start asking questions'

At the door she turned round. 'Stay put in the morning until I come to give you the all-clear.'

It was still half-light when he was wakened from a deep and satisfying sleep by a whisper and a hand stroking his hair out of his eyes. She smelt of warm milk and pine needles. 'There's a bite to eat,' she said, placing a bowl of milk and a hunk of bread on the small table next to the bed. Kyselak could not stop himself. He slipped his hand up her skirt as she leant forward. Before he could reach the silky softer skin of her thigh, however, he found his arm held in a surprisingly strong grip. He thought she was going to slap him for his presumption, but instead she placed her other hand gently over his mouth.

'Be quiet and eat your breakfast. I've got to get back or they'll wonder why I'm taking so long with the cows. I'll come and collect the things later, after my parents have set off for market.'

She had returned and slipped out of her loose dress and into the blankets with him. She was strong and energetic, full of pleasure and pleasure-giving. Kyselak was overwhelmed, almost intoxicated. It was his first time with a woman since the previous summer.

They lay back for a while in companionable silence, exhausted. Kyselak glanced at the figure stretched out beside him. He should ask her about herself, about her life here. He didn't even know her name, for God's sake! He was trying to work out a question that showed a genuine interest in milking cows and churning butter, but he was forestalled.

'Who's Katharina, then?'

Kyselak was flabbergasted. 'Who? But how …? What do you mean, Katharina?'

'Well at one point — when you probably didn't realise what you were saying — you cried out, "Oh Katharina, Katharina!" My name's Theresia, by the way. People call me Resi'

'Ah, Resi, yes … Josef, pleased to … I mean, I do apologise, I can't really explain it.' He saw a way out of his embarrassment. 'I suppose not knowing your name I just used one that came to mind. I do have a cousin of that name,' he added casually.

Of course, he could explain it, if he were honest with himself. Katharina had been appearing in his dreams, and more and more insistently of late. He told himself that because that strange evening with her had been his first experience with a woman, it was natural she should appear in his dreams as the object of his sexual urges. But there was more to it than that, even if he refused to admit it openly to himself.

When he had come home from his visit there two years ago his mother had kept on asking him about her, how he liked her, how they had got on together. She had even suggested inviting Katharina to stay with them in Vienna. Matrimony was as obviously in his mother's mind as it was absent from his own plans for the future. He had deliberately put aside his memories of his cousin and pretended a coldness which discouraged his mother from going through with the invitation.

Truth to tell, he had been a little frightened, or at least in awe of his cousin. If she had come to stay during the winter after his visit, he would probably have been as tongue-tied as the girls his mother's friends brought along when they came for their fortnightly helping of coffee, cakes and chit-chat.

Now, however, the way she came into his mind — and to his lips — unbidden suggested the memory of her was lodged deep within him. Some internal mechanism seemed to be determined to make it clear that she was the only girl he had met who meant more, who could mean more to him than a pleasant hour or two in bed. That there would be something missing from his life if she were not there.

But what would she say to his idea of spending every summer in the mountains? Something would be missing from his life without that, too. Would the love he was being forced to admit to be strong enough for him to sacrifice his wanderings to it? Was there the possibility of a life together for them? They were questions he couldn't answer, but what he could and would do was plan his next summer's trip to start in the Wachau, with a stop in Senftenberg, before going on to the Bohemian Forest.

Resi was gently massaging his chest. She smiled at him. 'No need to apologise. In fact most of the time — well, some of the time — I was thinking of my fiancé, Vinzenz. He's working for Count Morzin. For the last year he's been on the count's estates in Moravia. I haven't seen him since the New Year. We'll get married when we've saved enough to be able to take the lease of a farm. Or when my father decides to move in here.'

Her hand was gradually working its way down towards his stomach. 'Now, how about one more game of Vinzenz and Katharina before you go on your way?'

'Let me leave you then with this message: Lust is like a noxious weed that establishes itself and spreads if it is not rooted out when young; let us, therefore, accustom ourselves to curbing Lust in the smallest things so that it may not spread and choke the Divine Love that comes from Above. And what more appropriate time to put this resolve into practice than the New Year of 1820 which will so soon be upon us. In the Name of the Father, the Son and the Holy Ghost, Amen.'

4 A Haystack in Slovenia

Summer 1823/ 1820

Kyselak bent over the glass display case. *Lovage*: *The roots fresh dug up work by urine. The seeds have the same effect also and they dispel wind.* The botanical specimens brought back happy memories of his first walking tour and his cousin Katharina. And the geological cabinet had been very useful for checking the observations he had made during the last few weeks in the Steiner Alps. He had his own notes, of course, but he couldn't bring back samples in his knapsack. It was heavy enough with his spare clothes, food, telescope and notebooks. For the moment, though, he had had enough of looking at exhibits. The museum was very impressive, but the items in the display cases were starting to swim before his eyes. He sat down and thumbed through the brochure he had bought in the town.

A Description of the Remarkable and Instructive Museum known as the Johanneum in Graz, by Friedrich Schoberl.

> *The Johanneum takes its name from its founder, Archduke Johann. This prince, who has distinguished himself by his love of knowledge perhaps above any prince in Europe,*

and who is truly worthy of the high situation in which his birth has placed him, has pursued with unceasing assiduity an investigation into the resources both natural and political of Styria. He has himself surveyed every romantic scene, gathered every mountain-flower, estimated the capability of every rich valley, and drawn his conclusions as to what is excellent and what still remains to be improved. Wishing to make the stores of information he has collected of substantial use to the country, he determined to present his valuable collections and library to the inhabitants of the capital of the Province, that they might afford the means of instruction to the people and prove an encouragement to further research.

The Archduke accordingly gave the whole of this treasure, consisting of an herbal which contained fourteen thousand specimens, and a large store of minerals, an extensive library, philosophical instruments and manufactured products to the town of Graz. At this institution lectures are also advertised on 'mineralogy, botany, chemistry, astronomy, mechanics and the means of resuscitating persons apparently drowned ...'

Kyselak leant back and gazed at the agricultural display opposite. There were ploughs and spades, forks, scythes and sickles. And engravings showing them in use. Staring dreamily at the one illustrating different methods of haymaking throughout the Empire, he could almost smell the newly cut hay ...

Amid the oppressive heat the scent of freshly cut hay came to his nostrils. Beyond the trees was a small field, more hay-patch than hayfield, with half the grass cut and piled up to dry. The grass looked rather meagre, but as it was late August, it must be the *Krummet*, the second cutting.

He was weary with the heat, sweaty and thirsty. Tiny insects seemed to have crawled into every crevice of his body and he itched all over. He thought back with longing to the cool, emerald waters of the little shallow lake — what was it's name? Planschersee? something like that — surrounded by the steep sides of the Steiner Alps between Carinthia and Carniola. He had bathed there and, refreshed, slept soundly, wrapped in his blanket on the narrow strip of grass between the trees and the head of the lake. As he made his way up to the Seebergsattel the next morning he had painted the now obligatory KYSELAK, 1823 on a sheer rock face rising out of the trees above the water.

A sound caught his ear. Could that be running water? He pushed through the band of trees and scrub and felt the refreshing moistness even before he saw the small river. A little farther downstream it curved, forming a long pool. He went back to the edge of the wood and looked round. No one to be seen anywhere at all. It was only mid-afternoon, but perhaps they had given up haymaking for the day, or had to go back to milk the cows. Quickly he stripped off his clothes and slid into the water, feeling its cool caress run up his body until he plunged his head under and emerged, spluttering and shaking the drops out of his hair. He let himself drift down with the gentle current then, when it quickened over the shallows, swam the twenty yards back with vigorous strokes, revelling in the thrashing of his arms and legs against the water. He floated back down again, only his face above the surface, enjoying the mild heat of the leaf-veiled sun. Then he swam and dived and surfaced and rolled, kicking and splashing so that the drops rained down on him.

A rustling on the bank suggested a small mammal. Perhaps a water-rat come to join him? But the crack of a breaking twig brought his senses to the alert. That was a much heavier animal! His knapsack! He swam to the side and pulled himself out, just in time to see a figure slipping out of the trees. His knapsack and rifle had been stolen. And all his clothes! He set off after the thief, but the sharp branches on the ground and the briars in the undergrowth made progress slow. Thank God! The thief had dropped one of his boots. No, both of them. As he put them on, out of the corner of his eye he saw something slip behind the pile of hay in the field. When he emerged from the trees, he could see the miscreant's path clearly through the uncut grass. He thought of pulling off a spray of foliage to cover his nakedness, but alder leaves were no substitute for fig-leaves. Better to confront the thief naked than to have to seek help from a farm or — God forbid! — a village completely unclad.

He did pick up a dead branch, but as a weapon, and hurried through the grass. He rounded the stack of hay, club upraised, and stopped in astonishment. Sitting against the hay, clutching his knapsack and clothes, were two women, Slovene peasants by their dress. And, unlike thieves, they were giggling. He dropped his branch and quickly put his hand over his private parts, a male Venus rising from the waves of grass.

The two women — sisters? — said something, but it was beyond his rudimentary Slovene. '*Prosim?*' he ventured, but they just giggled again. After some more incomprehensible jabber, one took his shirt, the other his breeches and sat on them, defying him to reclaim his clothes. Except that the way their black skirts slipped back, revealing stretches of white thigh under a welter of even whiter petticoat, was anything but defiant. Inviting, rather. And the way the older one was stroking his rifle was highly suggestive. His body's instinctive response was inevitable and their giggles only increased as his hand could no longer cover his embarrassment.

There was a moment of stillness, then he threw himself on them. It was as much to put an end to his naked exposure as for any other reason, but the struggle that ensued quickly turned into something else as he found himself locked between the thighs of the younger woman. His thrusts became faster and more furious until, with a grunted 'Oh my God!' he flopped to the ground between the two, his face nestling in the new-cut hay.

He tried to work out what he could say, but then realised that, whatever it was, his Slovene would not be able to cope. He turned over on his back, gave a satisfied sigh and smiled at them in what he hoped was an appropriate manner. The older one — the mother, not the older sister? — then gave a most *un*satisfied sigh and a questioning look. Kyselak shrugged his shoulders and gestured towards his flaccid penis. She looked at him then smiled, a warm, almost motherly smile, and stretched out her arms towards him. He rolled over into her embrace, slipped a hand inside her loose bodice and laid his head on the pillow of her bosom, his lips brushing against the dark nipple.

She cradled him, and the buzzing of the insects was overlaid with a deeper resonance as she hummed a song that had the soothing contours of a lullaby. Unresisting, the drowsy Kyselak slid into the cocoon created by the rich vibrancy of sound, the humid heat and the sweet fragrance of the hayfield. Enveloped in softness and warmth, he was back in his childhood when illness merged the days into one long, hazy dream. The warmth was the fever, the softness the caress of the silk chemise his mother had let him wear to keep his sensitised skin from the roughness of the linen sheets. His mother put an extra eiderdown on top of him as well, to 'bring out' the fever. He could feel its gentle but insistent weight pressing down on him, wrapping itself round him, enfolding him. His whole body was suffused with a delicious heat. That was the fever collecting inside him, gathering its strength. It was going to break out, come to a climax, down there, oh yes ...

Kyselak woke to find himself looking up into the smiling face of his mother — no, of the older Slovene woman who enveloped him in the soft flesh of her arms, legs and breasts. And the smile on her face was definitely one of satisfaction.

Although it was late afternoon by now, the blanket of heat was still oppressive, made worse by the pieces of grass and insects sticking to their sweat-soaked bodies. The two women took off their dishevelled clothing, and all three plunged into the pool in the river, ducking and diving, laughing and spluttering as they pushed each other under the water.

Well, thought Kyselak, as he came out of his reverie in the Museum, they had certainly not needed the Archduke's lectures on resuscitating apparently drowned persons!

The portrait of Archduke Johann at the end of the room looked down on him benignly. If the stories about him were true, he would certainly approve of his romp with the Slovene women, perhaps even envy him for it. He had so far successfully resisted the dynastic marriage both the imperial family and Metternich were trying to foist on him. (He could almost hear his mother saying, 'Just like you Josef!') There were rumours that he was thinking of marrying a commoner. What was her name? Pickel? Plachl? Polster? Plochl, that was it. Kyselak could well imagine the Archduke following his emotions rather than protocol, but he could not imagine the Emperor ever allowing it. There had been some scandal during the War, something about the Archduke being involved in a secret scheme the Emperor did not know about. There had also been suggestions, nothing more, that some people planned to create a separate kingdom for Johann, to make him into a kind of King of the Alps.

Kyselak had no idea whether there was any truth in these rumours. To him the 'King of the Alps' sounded more like a character from one of the fairytale comedies that were popular in the Leopoldstadt Theatre. So little news was allowed to be published in Austria that rumour flourished. Whether the Archduke's publicly displayed loyalty to the Emperor sprang from a guilty conscience or genuine respect for his brother, the fact that for the last decade his energies had been almost entirely devoted to his province of Styria meant that the Empire had lost the services of the most able member of the Imperial family. But would the Archduke risk estranging himself even further by marrying a commoner?

Whatever the motivation of its founder, the Johanneum was an impressive institution. It was developing into a kind of university. Lectures on botany and chemistry, mineralogy and mechanics sounded more interesting than the arid benches of the philosophy faculty in Vienna. Perhaps he should take up his studies again, here in Graz? Study something more practical, something closer to his real interests? Botany and mineralogy would surely have retained his interest longer than the law he had abandoned after two years. Not that he had got much farther than the introductory philosophy courses. Studying in Graz was an attractive idea, but could he commit himself to it? Was his future not already settled? He couldn't disappoint his parents more than he had already done, especially after the efforts his father had made to find him his present position.

Kyselak still remembered the glacial atmosphere that had wrapped itself round the dining table when he announced, three years ago, that he was planning to abandon his studies at the university. The silence stretched to breaking point. His father continued to chew his roast chicken slowly and deliberately. By the time his mother let out a whispered, 'Oh, Josef ...' he must have reduced the meat to a smoother paste than even he, with his rigorous belief in proper mastication as a necessary preliminary to good digestion, demanded.

'You have, have you?'

'Yes, Father.'

'And why, might I ask?'

'Well, it ...' Kyselak paused. 'The lectures bore me to tears,' was not an answer that was likely to cut much ice with his father, despite the great emphasis he laid on telling the truth. 'Well, I'm not really learning anything. The lectures are just like someone reading from a book, and we're supposed to learn them off by heart so we can regurgitate them at the appropriate time. Even the classes with *Privatdozent* Novak are just cramming. We never discuss anything, it doesn't even seem to matter whether we understand it or not, as long as we can repeat what we've been taught. It's got even worse since Kotzebue was murdered and the authorities used that as an excuse to clamp down on students and professors. Almost everyone seems to be frightened of saying anything that might be reported to the police.'

His mother sighed. A glimmer of sympathy appeared in his father's eyes, but they quickly iced over again. 'Perhaps you would be so good as to tell us what you intend to do, then?'

'I want to be a writer.'

'You want to *be* a writer? Well, why not? One or two of the gentlemen in the ministry are writers. But what they *do* — to serve society and to earn their living — is work. Have you thought about that, or does work not come into your plans?'

'I thought perhaps I could continue to live here, with you … and use Uncle Alois's legacy until I've established myself. I can probably get some pieces in the newspapers and magazines to help pay for myself.'

'Ah, so it's a *scribbler* we want to be! And spend our days gossiping with other "writers" in the coffee houses, if not worse.' His father pushed his plate away from him, half finished, something unheard of from a man who believed wasting food was a sin against the holy spirit of practical reason.

'There's always my cabinet-making. Herr Veillich says I have good hands.'

'Cabinet-making as a hobby is one thing — if you must. But if you want to take it up professionally you will find you have to do an apprenticeship every bit as long and boring as your studies at the university. And setting up a workshop of your own is very costly — unless you plan to marry Veillich's daughter?'

Kyselak grimaced at the thought of the sharp-tongued shrew who seemed to hold a grudge against the whole world for her plain face, shapeless, flabby bosom and fat thighs.

'You are not attending university for your enjoyment,' his father went on. 'You are there to be trained, prepared, so that you can take up a responsible position in the world. If you want to develop your own ideas, your own philosophy, all well and good, but that is a private matter. Or at least,' he mused, almost to himself, 'it is nowadays. — If you want to know what routine is, what boredom is, you only need to do the work of those of us who have not had the privilege of attending university or do not enjoy the protection of some high-placed person. What I wouldn't give to have had your opportunities!'

Again he paused for reflection, staring at the tablecloth, presumably absorbed in the contemplation of what might have been. Then he raised his head, looked his son straight in the eyes and spoke slowly, enunciating each word separately:

'If you wish to continue to eat at this table, you will resume your studies in the autumn and continue them until you have qualified as a lawyer, or at least done enough to allow you to obtain a superior position with the chance of promotion. That I am willing to pay for, but not for some airy-fairy nonsense about *being* a writer.'

He stood up and went out, leaving Kyselak and his mother without a further word. She gave her son pleading looks as they listened to him take his hat, coat and stick and go out of the house, doubtless to join the *Stammtisch* of clerks and other minor civil servants in the Hungarian Crown tavern.

The chilly atmosphere had continued into the next week. Finally his mother found him a furnished room with the family of the housemaid of one of her friends. ('Very respectable people. The father had a good position with the Lower Austrian Insurance Company until he fell ill. Since then the mother and daughter have had to work their fingers to the bone to keep their heads above water.') The meagre allowance she could manage to make him from her own money and what she could save out of the housekeeping would just about cover his expenses. So one late spring morning he had put his clothes, books and a couple of pieces of furniture he had made himself into a cart and left his parents' home, clutching the manuscript of his tragedy, *The Last Knight*, to him. 'Like a girl holding her bastard child as her father tells her never to darken his doorstep again,' he thought, though the image was rather spoilt by the fact that his father had already left for the office.

As soon as summer arrived, he had set off for the hills, financing the journey from the small legacy he had received from his Uncle Alois. Once he returned in the autumn it would be more or less all gone, but he intended to enjoy his summer and leave thinking about how to earn a living until he was back in Vienna. He was heading for the Bohemian Forest, but there was an important visit he intended to make on the way.

Kyselak tramped along the lanes and footpaths on the north bank of the Danube. It was a bright day and the woods and fields were busy with life but, unusually for him, he had no eye for the profusion of flowers, no ear for the tumult of birdsong around him. His head was full of images of his cousin Katharina which swirled round in his mind, stopped and came to life for a moment, only to dissolve into others, like the patterns in the kaleidoscope that was all the rage at the moment in Vienna.

Ever since he had unwittingly exclaimed — no, ejaculated, that was the word — her name last summer, he had spent much of his time daydreaming about Katharina, imagining scenes from a life together which were gradually taking on the texture of real memory. And, of course, each one ended with vividly pictured, passionate lovemaking.

She didn't accompany him on his long treks, but otherwise they did everything together. She even climbed the mountains with him, as confident and sure-footed over the rocks as he was. One of their first outings remained a special memory, even if a memory of a daydream. They had spent the night snuggled cosily together in a hay-barn above Hirschwang in the Höllental, then set off up the Rax first thing in the morning. They were following the 'Gateway Path' which ended in a natural rock portal leading onto the top. The only problem was, they couldn't see it. Everywhere was wrapped in mist that obscured vision and deadened sound. It was an eerie climb, as if their ears were blocked and their eyes veiled with mucus, but they managed to find the Gateway and set off along the ridge. The first sign of change was a warmth which took the chill off the damp air, then it gradually grew brighter until, finally, they stepped out of the clutches of the mist into the dazzling sunshine of a cloudless sky. They were standing on an island in a billowing sea of white foam, the other peaks — the Schneeberg, the Schneealpe, the Hohe Veitsch, the Hochschwab — dotted around them like a rocky archipelago. For a long time they stared, arms round each other, into the silent splendour, the only human beings in this pristine world. Then they sank to the ground and into each other, closer than they had ever been, one flesh in the primal harmony of nature. — And of course the one — the only? — advantage of a daydream was that rocks and stones don't stick into your back.

He kept telling himself to keep a grip on reality, to save his fantasies for his poetry, but his imagination had always been

59

stronger than reason and the image of Katharina had taken hold of his mind. He had lived through a whole life with her in his imagination and he kept revisiting favourite scenes, adding a touch here, changing a detail there with all the meticulousness of a biographer. Would he be able to blank out this 'knowledge' when he met her and revert to being the cousin who had spent one night with her and her mother three years ago and 'just happened to be passing' again?

But his fantasy world was so delightful, and so fulfilling. They walked together, they made love, but they also lived and worked together. Kyselak had brought out a slim volume of verse and Katharina had found a publisher keen to take the family herbal she was compiling. On their summer trips he helped her collect her specimens while she declaimed his poems to him, changing an image here, improving a rhyme there. And in the winter they sat either side of the warm stove, each involved in their own work, yet always conscious of the other.

'Sepperl, look at this gentian.' She held out a little dried flower. 'Do you remember where we found it?' Her voice was deep, her smile enticing.

'You mean that grassy depression surrounded by rocks we came across by chance, Kathi, when we were trying to creep up on the chamois?'

'Some chance, with the clatter of your boots on the rocks! But you said the grass was as soft as any cushions and the warm rocks made it just like sitting by the stove at home and —'

'— and then we ...' but already they were on the floor, piling up the cushions in the angle of the stove, already he was kicking off his slippers, throwing his jacket to the ground, already Kathi's loose *peignoir* had slipped open ...

If only the world were like that! A world where he was appreciated for what he was, inside, not for how he appeared on the outside, a failed student with little money and less prospects. The world he dreamed up, where they had the *entrée* of Vienna's literary salons. They even had a nickname as a couple, *utile cum dulce*, the couple who combined practical knowledge of nature with its transfiguration in poetry. And doors would open!

'Herr Kyselak? I've just been talking to your wife. Delightful lady and so learned in her subject! I have a proposal that might interest you. A, er, gentleman — I will name no names at the moment, but you can rest assured he is highly placed, *most* highly placed — well, this gentleman is looking for someone to act as curator for his library and scientific collections. It is a task that requires taste and learning as well as a modicum of scientific knowledge and an elegant style. We thought that you, assisted by your so capable wife ...'

Would he ever find fulfilment outside his daydreams? In the distance he could see a ruined tower on the hill. It was the place where he had written his name, KYSELAK 1817, in the euphoria of his first visit. He was already approaching Senftenberg! He would have to make an effort to put all his fantasies out of his mind, or at least lock them up in some dark corner. Otherwise he might respond to the real Katharina by a look, a gesture, a word, as if she were the creature his imagination had constructed, as if the relationship between them were something much closer than that of two cousins who had met only once before.

As he approached the house, still surrounded by a blaze of geraniums, hollyhocks and paeonies, he thought back to the visit of three years ago, when he was still a schoolboy, startled and thrilled by their furtive fumblings under the cover of the massive oak table. He was well beyond that now. Her tall, lithe figure, her self-assurance, her stern look and the way it had once softened as she glanced at him, the way the back of her hand had stroked his cheek as she placed his bowl of coffee on the table in front of him ... This had all crystallised in his mind into an ideal of womanhood, *his* ideal of womanhood. It was about to be confronted with reality. Did he really want that? Better the dream than the certain knowledge? No. He had taken one step — quitting the university — which, whether it turned out to be a mistake or not, was his own decision. He had to face up to reality, whatever it might bring.

Though arriving unannounced, he was given a warm welcome. His aunt was as chatty as ever. 'Well, this is a nice surprise, isn't it, Katharina? How long is it since you came to see us? Three years it must be. Three more years without my poor, dear husband ... But we mustn't be sad when we have such a welcome visitor. You'll find things have changed since you were last here. Now that times are a bit better the Baron has finished restoring the tower, you can see it from the window there. You did go and have a look at it last time, didn't you? Even wrote your name on it, you scamp. KYSELAK — in capital letters. It gave me quite a shock when I saw it. Ah well, boys will be boys ...'

Katharina was her usual stern self. He couldn't tell whether she was pleased to see him or wished he hadn't come back. 'You can have the same room, but as you didn't warn us you were coming it'll take some time to get ready. Don't bother to get up, I can manage by myself. You just sit there and talk to Mother while I get the sheets aired and make up the bed. '

The next day he accompanied her on a botanical ramble. — 'To see what there is to see and to gather some things for the evening meal.' — As he walked beside her, carrying the basket for specimens and the bag with some slices of marble cake ('In case you get peckish. My late husband always used to take a few slices with him when he went out hunting. It was his favourite cake. He always used to say ...') Katharina kept up a constant stream of information about what they could see and smell.

'There, lime flowers! Isn't that a heady smell?! This is just the right time. We're going to gather them on Friday. Several of us get together to collect them along the avenue. We get ladders and some of the boys climb up. They wouldn't let me! And then I dry them. They make a lovely infusion ...'

He was glad he wasn't required to respond, except for the occasional, 'Oh, yes,' or 'Yes, it's lovely.' His thoughts had gone back to his previous visit and the astonishing experience that had been. He watched his cousin bend down,

'— Oh, chamomile. The best tea there is. And I use it to make a lotion for washing my hair. But it's a little early yet. We have plenty left at home still —'

and the sight of her lithe body, a little fuller now than he remembered, plus the memory of the evening in the candle-lit room while her mother dozed over her embroidery, triggered off the first stirrings of lust in his loins. She hurried on ahead into some open woodland

'Look, here's Turk's cap lilies. Aren't they beautiful? Such a deep purple! People dig them up to plant in their gardens. But they also dig them up for the bulbs. They're very yellow. On the farms higher up the valley they call them golden apples and wear them as amulets against the evil eye. The young folk use them as love charms. Shall I get you one to take back to Vienna?'

She turned to him, a mischievous sparkle in her eyes which

took his breath away. Then she suddenly hurried past him to a tree covered in creamy-white blossom.

'Ah, there it is! That's what I was looking for. Elderflowers. Just smell them. Isn't that a rich, sweet scent?' She came up close to him and held the flowers under his nose. Was that the scent of the elderflowers that filled his nostrils, or the smell of her hair, her skin?

'We'll have some elderflower fritters tonight after dinner. I'll make them myself once Marie's finished. You just dip them in batter, fry them and eat them with sugar. Delicious! Come on. You can reach higher than me. Help me get some.'

He plucked one or two, then stared at her as she reached up. The desire he felt had disappeared, or rather been overlaid by something else, absorbed into a much stronger feeling that enveloped his whole body, his whole being. Just to be with this woman, so supple, so sure of herself, so lively, yet so serious, to be with her always —

'Don't just stand there. How many flower heads have you got? Three? You're not going to get much of a helping tonight, if you don't look lively.'

He came out of his trance and clambered up onto a rock to collect some particularly fine-looking flowers near the top of the tree. As he jumped down and tossed them into the basket, she said, 'There's a nice grassy bank by a little stream just up here. We can rest and have a drink — and eat some of that marble cake. Just the thing when you're out for a walk, as my father used to say,' she added with a smile and a wink.

After they had drunk from the stream and finished off the cake, they stretched out on the grass. Katharina did not pull away when his head came up against her thigh. Kyselak lay back, looked

64

at the clouds scudding slowly across the sky and sighed contentedly.

After a while — how long? — he felt her fingers ruffling his hair. He turned over and hauled himself up on his elbows to look her in the face, but she was gazing up at the sky. With a groan of 'Katharina,' he cuddled up to her and she cradled him, like a mother cradling her child. But when he placed his hand on her firm breast, she took it away, gently, and half sat up, still holding him in her arms.

'Oh Josef,' she said, and for a long while she said nothing else. Then, as if she were explaining something to a child, she went on, 'You're a nice boy, but ... but anyway, it's too late. I'm already promised to another. I'm going to marry Karl in the spring. When he moves into the forester's house on Count Heberstein's estate. It's all arranged, only we haven't told Mother yet. Once she knows, she'll talk of nothing else. I suppose it would make a change of subject matter from my poor old father, but I can't face the idea of her going on for ten months about me and Karl and the marriage and the trousseau and who's going to be invited to the wedding. We're going make it a kind of Christmas present for her.'

At his crestfallen look, she said, 'Come now, it can't be that bad. I don't believe you've been harbouring a white-hot passion for me for the last three years. There must be plenty of nice girls in Vienna —'

An expression of disgust appeared on his face, and she hurriedly went on, 'Yes, I know very well it's not a "nice little girl" that you want. Do you want to get married at all? What time will you have for a woman in your life if you spend all summer wandering the mountains and the rest of the year wrestling with your verse tragedy? I can't see anyone who's not the archetypal "little woman" standing for that.'

She stood up and held out her hand to pull him up. Placing a chaste kiss on his lips, she said, 'Promise me you'll come to the wedding? You'll like Karl. You can talk about your mountains and forests with him. He even has a jotter full of poems — well, just rhymes really. He composes them while he's out working in the forests by himself, but I soon put any fancy ideas out of his head. "If you think reciting poems to your trees makes them happier," I told him, "then carry on. But when you come home I expect you to bring me a brace of pheasants or plump rabbits, not a sonnet to the nightingale."'

Kyselak spent that summer in the mountains of the Bohemian Forest, as planned. For a while he sought out empty places, going down to the villages for supplies as seldom as possible. The emptiness that was inside him remained, but was gradually masked by a melancholy which even had a certain sweetness. He cultivated it, eventually taking a kind of pleasure in what he saw as his fate as 'The Wanderer'. And he had to admit it proved not unattractive to a certain class of Czech dairymaid …

When he returned to Vienna, late in the autumn, he discovered that his father had spent the summer seeing people and using what little influence he had to obtain him the position of clerk in the Court Chamber. It was a minor post, and not one that promised a great future, but at least it gave him enough to live on and time to devote to his writing during the winter.

He had not gone back to live in his parents' house, though he took meals there regularly. He even talked with his father, discussing happenings in their respective ministries and what news the papers were allowed to print. Two serious men putting the world to rights.

He had thought of finding himself another room. An attic, a garret, something like that. He had visions of himself on dark winter evenings, the rain lashing against the windowpanes, huddled up in his bedclothes for warmth, counting out the feet of his verses on the almost-cold tiles of the stove. (Goethe had done it on his lover's spine, but then he wasn't Goethe, nor ever would be.) In the end, however, he stayed with Frau Smutny. She spoiled him almost as much as his mother did, but then why not? Physical discomfort was not a *sine qua non* of poetic composition, he told himself. The emptiness that remained in his heart where the image of Katharina had been was suffering enough.

As he came out of the Museum and made his way across the main square of Graz, beneath the precipitous bulk of Castle Hill, he was in reflective mood. Seeing Archduke Johann's collection of samples and artefacts connected with all aspects of his homeland had made him think. Perhaps he should consider writing something more practical? As well as his poetry, of course, that fulfilled a deep-seated need, he could not give that up. But if his love of nature and the countryside could be transmuted into poetry, was there any reason why it should not at the same time provide the material for a more down-to-earth work? A description of the things he had seen and experienced on his walking tours, the people he had met, their customs, their stories and songs? It would probably have more chance of getting published than his poems or his tragedy. At least his father would understand and approve, and it might even bring him to the notice of some aristocratic patron like the Archduke. Katharina might be lost for ever, but he could think of her as his muse — Urania rather than Melpomene — as he made notes on the flora and fauna, the rock formations and watercourses he observed on his travels. Continuing on his way, he hummed a folk song to himself:

> The time has come when we must part,
> My love, my own true dear.
> 'When will you come again, my heart?'
> When darkly ends the year.

5. A Letter from Gastein

To:
Herr Ferdinand Schubert
Vienna.
Steyr, 21st September, 1825

Dear Brother,

Following your request I will try to give you a detailed description of our journey to Salzburg and Gastein. You know I have no gift for words, but since I will have to tell you everything when we return to Vienna anyway, I prefer to send you a written sketch of the beauties we have seen on our travels. However feeble it turns out to be, it will certainly be better than an oral account.

We left Steyr around the middle of August and drove to Kremsmünster. I have often seen it before but the situation is so beautiful I cannot bear to miss it out. The extensive monastery on a prominent hill rising above a delightful valley forms a magnificent view from the road, particularly enhanced by the Astronomical Tower. There seemed to be an inscription on the side facing the road, which I had not noticed on previous visits. To my weak eyes it was just a hazy jumble but Vogl, who prides himself on his keen eyesight, though it is not a lot better than mine, said it appeared to begin with a 'K' and be followed by some number. A date? 'Kaiser'? 'Kremsmünster'? Our welcome was so warm, we forgot to ask. We have been known here for some years — Herr von Vogl even studied here — and were very kindly received. However, we did not stay, but continued our journey as far as Vöcklabruck. It is a wretched hole, no more need be said.

The next day we continued into the province of Salzburg, where the houses have a very distinctive architecture. Nearly everything is of wood. Wooden kitchen utensils stand on wooden trestles beneath the wooden galleries running round the wooden walls of the houses. And everywhere there are targets still bearing the marks of the shots that struck them, kept as trophies of victories in shooting matches won long ago. They often bear a date of 1600, or even 1500.

The countryside around is amazingly beautiful, the bright green waters of the Wallersee come right up to the road. This part is quite high up and from here on the land drops gradually down to the city of Salzburg. It was like driving through the garden of Eden, except that we had one advantage over paradise, namely that we were sitting in a comfortable coach, a convenience denied to Adam and Eve. And instead of wild beasts we encountered many charming girls.

However, I must not give the wrong impression of the excellent inhabitants of the area. Vierthaler, in his Geography of Salzburg, which Herr von Vogl borrowed from our friends in Steyr, says, 'The results of their varied industry can be seen not only in their prosperity, but also in the high degree of morality which distinguishes the inhabitants of these mountainous regions from others. Murder, theft, robbery and fraud they know of but by name. If a crime of that kind is ever committed, the perpetrator nearly always turns out to be a vagrant stranger.'

In the meanest farmhouse everywhere here you find window-frames and door-posts of marble, and even sometimes stairs of red marble.

The sun darkened and, like troubled spirits, thick clouds veiled the black mountains beyond the city. But they did not touch the brow of the legendary Untersberg, they crept past as if in awe of Emperor Barbarossa asleep in his cave deep inside the mountain.

In Salzburg we were introduced, through Herr Pauernfeind, a merchant well known to Herr von Vogl, to Count von Platz, whose family made us most welcome. Vogl sang some of my songs, whereupon we were invited for the following evening and asked to perform an assortment of our things before a select circle. The way in which Vogl sings and I accompany him, as though we were one, is something quite new and unheard-of for these people ...

So we left Salzburg and continued our journey at a comfortable pace, lost in delight at the fine day and the still finer country, in which no one particular object arrested our attention except for a pretty building called the 'Month's Castle' because an archbishop had it built within a month for his fair lady. Everyone knows this here, but no one is shocked by it. What charming tolerance!

A few hours later we reached the curious but extremely dirty and horrid town of Hallein. The inhabitants all look like ghosts, pale, hollow-eyed and shrivelled enough to catch fire. The contrast of such a rat-hole with the delightful valley surrounding it left me with a dismal feeling. It was as though we had fallen from heaven into a dung-heap or, after listening to Mozart's music, were now confronted with a piece by the immortal A. There was no way of inducing Vogl to visit the salt mines there. Like a lonely wanderer drawn to a point of light in the darkness, that great soul, spurred on by his gout, had his sights set firmly on Gastein, that wild watering place whose healing properties have been known for over a thousand years.

You particularly asked me for a detailed description of Gastein. I will not attempt to describe the town itself, other artists have done that, but the transition from bright sunshine to darkest night, from the

71

blessings of peace into the warring elements, made an impression that will never leave me.

It was evening when we arrived there. The golden waves of the sun were still surging round the peaks above as we stepped onto the bridge over Gastein's gorge. Cliffs, tall and black, the harbingers of darkness, hemmed us in on all sides, redoubling the din of the stream rushing down beneath us. With a seething, tearing, thunderous roar, the raging stream leaps down three eighty-foot steps, whipping itself up against the hard rocks into a witches' cauldron then, with a fury that mocks even volcanoes, sweeping the exhausted waves away. The quivering of the jagged rocks, the impact of the irate waters, sending heavy drops of rain, in an inversion of nature, over the huts and back up to the clouds, the darkness of the sunless gorge, veiled by the vapours rising from the hot springs, and finally the little houses, swaying like water-mills, clutching precariously to individual rocks, unsure whether they will still be there on the morrow — all this may well send the curious stranger into raptures, but can hardly be calculated to comfort the sick such as Herr von Vogl, who came seeking repose and relief from his gout.

As we were about to go back to the town and our lodgings, we had a strange encounter. I heard someone singing one of my songs! In a loud and rather tuneless voice, but still recognisable: 'From mountains high and lone I come, / By raging streams unlit by sun, / I wander on, weighed down by care …' Then the singer appeared, coming round the corner from the valley above Gastein. He was a young man, about the same age as myself, but unshaven, his skin ruddy from exposure to wind and weather. His clothes were crumpled, torn and dirty, as if he had been sleeping in them. With his knapsack on his back and rifle in his hand, he looked like one of those 'vagrant strangers' Vierthaler talks about. Yet he was singing one of my songs! With feeling, if a

72

little flat. As he passed, he gave Vogl and me a look of deepest contempt, as if we were the criminals, not him. He then stood on the bridge, contemplating the scene that had so moved me just a few moments before, ignoring us completely. I would have been interested to know how such a disreputable-looking figure came to be singing my Wanderer, but the back he had turned towards us seemed to exude hostility, and we returned to our lodgings ...

  God keep you safe until you are embraced again by your

loving brother,

Franz

P.S. This will be delivered by hand. There isn't anything in it that will threaten to engulf the state in bloody revolution, but I prefer not to think of one of Sedlnitzky's monkeys getting his sticky paws on it. Erich Otto Nemetz, one of Herr von Vogl's friends, is going to Vienna tomorrow and has kindly offered to take care of any papers we would like to entrust to him. — F.

6. *The Mill and the Archduke*

Summer 1826

Kyselak looked down at the adder. Another step and he might have trodden on it, or frightened it away. As it was, it seemed unconcerned, curled up on its cushion of moss between the rocks, its body slightly flattened to catch as much of the heat of the sun as possible.

Following the animal's example, he settled himself down comfortably in the warm grass. It was a beautiful creature, a rich mustardy brown with chocolate brown markings down its back, the gloss of its skin suggesting it had recently sloughed. A female — males were generally greenish-grey and black — and probably pregnant. They had regular sites where they came day after day to absorb the energy from the sun as the young developed inside them. The males were vagabonds. At least whenever he had come across one it had been busily nosing its way through the undergrowth.

Was it the same with human beings? Once the warm weather came he was always visited by a restless urge to leave the city and explore the countryside. And he certainly felt no desire to settle down in a warm little nest with one of those girls his mother insisted on inviting to her 'afternoons'. The male and female adders as symbols of human behaviour? Perhaps he could use it in a poem. He looked down at the snake again. *Curled up on her mossy bed/ Receptive to the warming sun/ Whose rays di-dah-di-dah her eggs* ... Could you rhyme eggs with bed? Perhaps. But didn't adders give birth to live young, in which case he couldn't use the rhyme anyway. And the male? *Gliding through the waving grass/ Over rocks, 'neath gorse and briar/ Ever searching, ever striving* ... 'Waving grass' was a bit of a cliché, and 'striving' was too human, too obvious, but it was enough to give the basic concept. He jotted it down in his 'ideas book'. He might be able to work it up into something for one of the annual literary anthologies such as *Aurora*, though the editors would probably feel an adder as a subject for a poem would be offputting to their many lady subscribers. Still, it was worth trying.

He took out his telescope and looked at the mill down in the valley. The shepherds in the alpine pasture the night before last had described the miller's widow who owned it as 'hospitable'. He hadn't been able to tell whether they were hinting at something more than just a willingness to give a traveller a bite to eat and a bed in the barn. Partly it was their accent, of course, but they were so plain and open in their speech that a *risqué sous-entendu* seemed completely beyond them.

Why was it that watermills always seemed to inspire poets to artless lyrics? Like shrinking violets and roses 'mid the heather. And nightingales. Or the moon of course. Even trout! But no one had yet written a poem about an adder, as far as he knew. Nor about a tick, he thought, as he picked off the one crawling up his trousers and squashed it between his thumbnails. Not surprisingly, perhaps. Though Goethe had done one about a flea. A poem about a tick would obviously have to be satirical too.

And that meant it would never be published. But it was quite a nice idea: the censor as a tick on the beautiful body of Art. And the red ink he used on manuscripts the blood he sucked from the body of Art. No, just a minute, you didn't see the blood until the tick had been crushed, and unfortunately there was no hope of that happening to the censors. The red ink as the marks the tick/ censor had left after sucking the lifeblood from Art. Something along those lines. It was worth trying to develop it, even if it had to join his Winkelried poem in the secret hiding place. He could see himself working on it when he needed something to relieve his frustrations.

Everything was quiet at the mill. None of the busy clatter of the mill-wheel so beloved of poets. He hoped it wasn't as deserted as it looked. After five nights spent under the stars or in draughty, smoky mountain huts, he would like a warm bed. Even if he had to make do with empty flour-sacks, at least there would be no smell of cow dung or wood smoke. And the thought of a hot meal made his stomach cry out. It was a beautiful day, he could sit by the river until someone turned up. Perhaps he'd even catch a trout or two. That poem had described a clever trick ...

Filled with pleasant anticipation, he sang to himself as he swung down the grassy slope to the mill:

> Down in a shady valley
> The river turns a mill.
> There lived my darling Sally,
> Oh, that she lived there still!
>
> A ring of gold she gave me
> And vowed she'd e'er be true.

How soon that vow was broken,
The gold ring cleft in two.

A wand'rer now, I —

No, that was a bit pessimistic for his present mood. And anyway, he was heading *for* the mill, not out into the wide, cruel world. He wanted something a bit happier, a bit more optimistic:

Oh, I see a mill-wheel gleaming
'mid the alder's green leaves,
The busy waters singing
Their sweet melodies

How my heart leaps at the mill wheel's
Blithe and welcoming song ...

That was more like it. Though everyone knew how that particular welcome had ended ...

Apart from the occasional creak of machinery, it was as quiet inside the mill as outside. Kyselak looked round. A plain room, the wood of the floor, walls and ceiling dark with age. A table stood in one corner, next to the door into an adjoining room. Against the wall opposite was a smaller table with a jug on it full of wild flowers. They were still fresh, probably only gathered that morning by the look of them, so there must be people around somewhere near. On the wall above the flowers were three mounted chamois heads, and on the wall opposite the entrance was the *Herrgottswinkel* with the crucifix and below it a crudely painted picture of a saint in fervent prayer. Underneath the picture was a shelf and a shallow bowl with a candle stub.

The one surprising object in the room was what appeared to be a map of the Empire hanging over the desk. Kyselak took a step to have a closer look then stopped as the old floorboards creaked. Even though he appeared to be alone in the building, he felt embarrassed at causing a noise, so he tiptoed towards the desk. Then he stopped again. The creak of machinery, louder this time. Except ... Except that the mill wasn't operating, and the machinery was surely on the other side of the building, anyway. That creaking sounded suspiciously like a bed —

'Stop! Murder! Assassin!'

In surprise at the sudden shout, Kyselak tripped over a stool and slid along the waxed and polished floor until he was brought to a stop by his head hitting the wall with a loud crack. As he fell, he let go of his rifle, which went off — again! — but not, as far as he could tell, injuring anyone. At least, he wasn't injured and no one else cried out.

He must have blacked out for a few seconds, perhaps even more. When he came to, he saw the door to the other room open. Less than a yard from his face a pair of bare feet appeared. Through the legs he could see a woman pulling some kind of gown tight round her and cowering against the bed as if she were afraid the mill had been invaded by the Cossack army bent on rape and pillage.

'What is the meaning of this, Zahlbruckner? Not taking an easy pot at some chamois, are you? Not very sporting.' An arm was raised and pointed at the mounted heads.

'No, sir. I just went out — call of nature, you know —'

'And fell asleep again?'

'I sat in the sun by the river for a while and when I came back —'

The speaker must have pointed at Kyselak, for the feet took a step backwards and a face, a vaguely familiar face, looked down at him.

Kyselak levered himself up on his elbows, trying to remember where he had seen that face, forgot about the desk, knocked his head, already aching from contact with the wall, against it and fell down again. The man addressed as Zahlbruckner came over and helped him up.

Kyselak quickly tried to make amends. 'I do apologise, your honour. I thought there was no one in here, I thought perhaps they were through there in the mill. I did knock and call out before I came in. The door was open —' The man, who was stuffing his shirt back into his trousers, gave Zahlbruckner a glance. 'I've been sleeping out under the stars for the last week, or in huts in the mountains, and I was hoping I might find a bed here for the night, or a place to sleep in the barn.'

'So you're not a member of some revolutionary secret society come to murder us in our beds?'

'No, sir, of course not, sir. I'm sorry about the shot, but this gentleman' — Kyselak gestured towards Zahlbruckner — 'surprised me and I tripped. It was fortunate that no one was injured. Nor any serious damage done,' he said, looking up at the massive beam in the ceiling where the ball had lodged. 'Perhaps you could make the bullet into a kind of family legend. "The night the French troops stormed the mill" ... or something like that,' he added lamely when he saw that his attempt at humour was falling on barren ground. 'I'm on a walking tour for the summer.'

'So you're not a journeyman miller looking for work, either?'

'No, your honour, I'm a clerk in the Court Chamber, though I have to admit my dress does look more like that of a travelling journeyman. I like to spend my summers —' Kyselak stopped. He had suddenly realised why the man's face was familiar. Surely he had seen his portrait in Graz a couple of years ago. 'I do apologise, Your Imp—'

The man broke in. 'Brandhofer, the name's Brandhofer.'

'Of course, Your ... Herr von Brandhofer, sir. Kyselak, Josef Kyselak at your service, sir.' Kyselak clicked his heels gently and bowed.

'Kyselak ... Kyselak? The name sounds familiar. I'm sure I've seen it somewhere. Have we met before? No, I thought not. Are you a writer? Have I read something by you?'

'No, sir. Or, if it is not tempting fate, not *yet*, sir. I am working on a book at the moment and I hope it may appear soon.'

'Not another tragedy, I trust? All you young men seem to want to write is tragedies. Life can be sad enough as it is.' A shadow passed over the man's face, but quickly dispersed.

'No sir. I am *also* writing a tragedy, about your ancestor — I mean about Emperor Maximilian I. But the book I am talking about is an account of my travels in 1825. I walked right through the mountains, from Styria to Carinthia, Salzburg and Tyrol. I am trying to describe both the things I have seen and the people I have met, mostly simple farmers and shepherds. This present journey is in part an attempt to gather some additional material to supplement the notes I made last year.'

'Are you now? You sleep out in the open? And travel alone? Without guides?'

'Yes ... er ... sir. I'm quite experienced at finding my way now. I do ask the local people for advice, but they often want to take the quickest, safest route, while I like to go to the mountain tops, to stop and enjoy the view. I also like to spend some time examining the rocks and the flora.'

'This sounds fascinating. You must tell me more.' Archduke Johann — yes, that was definitely who it was, despite the alias — seemed to have forgotten he was barefoot and that part of his shirt was still sticking out of his breeches. 'Zahlbruckner,' he said, turning to his companion, 'go to the kitchen and see if Josefa has recovered from the shock. Get her to give us some food. Bread, some of that smoked pork and a large portion of her hazelnut *Strudel*.' He smiled at Kyselak. 'I'm sure Herr Kyselak — Kyselak, hmm? With a 'y'? I've definitely seen that name somewhere — anyway, I'm sure he has a healthy appetite after all those days in the mountains. Take that table and three chairs outside for us. It's a balmy evening and Herr Kyselak can show us which mountains he crossed.'

Kyselak went to help Zahlbruckner, but the Archduke stopped him. 'Zahlbruckner can manage himself. He's just a stripling, a whole month younger than I am. And being my secretary, he's used to working with tables. Come and show me where you've been.'

With that the Archduke pushed his bare feet into a pair of felt slippers kept on a shelf by the door and went out onto the wooden terrace outside the mill-house.

Kyselak pointed to the massive bulk of the Totes Gebirge to the north-east. 'I visited the monastery in Admont, then went by the Pyhrn Pass, over the Warscheneck to Hinterstoder and from there I climbed the Großer Priel. The last few days I have been making my way down through the Totes Gebirge. I observed the mill from up there.' Kyselak pointed to the slope where he had seen the snake. 'It looked very inviting after five days in the wild.' He smiled apologetically.

'You got to the top of the Priel? I and my companion tried it from this side, with a huntsman to guide us, but the weather was bad and unfortunately we had to turn back.'

While they were talking of paths and peaks, Zahlbruckner brought out the table and three chairs. A woman appeared with a large tray — presumably the woman who had been afraid the Cossacks were about to launch into rape and pillage — and set out food and wine on the table. The Archduke motioned Kyselak to a chair and Zahlbruckner joined them.

'Nowadays the appreciation of nature is becoming quite widespread among the population in general. It's even a kind of fashion in some circles, artists, musicians and that kind of thing,' the Archduke said. 'Not that I've anything against artists and musicians, but I'm more of a practical man myself. What I mean to say is that people go on excursions and walking tours in the country, but it is unusual, not to say unique, to meet someone who visits the wildest places by himself, someone who is willing to brave the dangers and the inclement weather, not to mention abandoning the comforts of a warm bed and good cooking. I know that for centuries hunters and farmers, shepherds and dairymaids have gone into the mountains when their business takes them there, and I do not want to belittle what they do. But what I think is important is that a man of education, such as yourself, should go there and then come back and describe what he has seen. Having to rely on yourself so much must mean you come into close, intimate contact with the landscape, so to speak. Is that what you are writing about in your book?'

'I hope to give my readers — if the book is ever published — a sense of the beauty and grandeur of our country. I do not expect that many will actually follow me onto the mountain ridges and peaks, but I hope they will be better able to appreciate what they see from afar. I think an increase in the number of visitors will be very important if the towns and villages, many of which at the moment are well off the beaten track, are to develop into modern communities with lively industrial and commercial activities.'

'Yes, that is very important. As you probably know, and for reasons we need not go into' — Archduke Johann was obviously forgetting or abandoning his Herr von Brandhofer persona — 'for many years now I have concentrated my efforts on improving the lot of our citizens in my province of Styria. I have set up my farm, the *Brandhof*, as a model to encourage agricultural improvement throughout the region. And if the farmers are to improve their stock and increase their yields, they must have a market to sell their surplus produce. More visitors from the cities will provide part of that market, which will allow the farmers to buy more of the amenities of modern civilisation and improve their soil and equipment.'

The Archduke grew eloquent, his rather thin cheeks flushed with enthusiasm. Occasionally appealing to Zahlbruckner for supporting facts or figures, he described his wide-ranging activities to develop the economy of Styria: the factory for making machinery that he had bought, the farmers' association he had set up, the savings bank and the fire insurance union he had founded, the roads and bridges he had had built or improved.

'I see all these things not as separate enterprises, but as part of a whole. And the key is education, of which things like your book will form a valuable part. If Styria, if the Empire itself is to take its place in the modern world, then our economy and society must be put on a modern basis —'

The Archduke broke off and gave Kyselak a quizzical look. 'I'm getting quite carried away. I hope you're not one of Metternich's spies? An *agent provocateur* sent to tempt me into saying things I shouldn't? Of course you aren't. Metternich's parasites will do many things, but I think that tramping round the country in torn trousers, wearing boots that have all too clearly been frequently soaked and' — the Archduke pointed at the plates, which Kyselak was surprised to see were empty — 'going hungry are not part of them. I have to say — in the strictest confidence, of course — that my brother is a little suspicious of anything that threatens the *status quo*. But this quite natural hesitancy with regard to change is shamelessly abused by those around him. When he says, "Anyone who comes along with new ideas can leave, or I will see to it that he is sent packing," it is not my brother I hear but a certain prince.'

The Archduke stood up and addressed his companion, who had been fidgeting impatiently for some time. 'Yes, I know Zahlbruckner, I am being indiscreet and we must be on our way. Goodbye, Herr Kyselak, it has been a pleasure talking to you. I hope to read your book soon. I'm sure Josefa will find you a comfortable bed and a warm meal so that you can continue on your journey of discovery refreshed.'

7. *Theatrical Aspirations*

Winter 1827-8

> — *Herr von Reich is in great danger! You must go and help him at once!*
> — *But what about my dear father! All his money is lost. I fear he may do himself an injury!*
> — *Herr von Reich is the only man who can save your father's fortunes. The machinations of the evil count have left him on the brink of disaster! You must go and rescue him. Go!*

Bonafay The Good Fairy waved her magic wand. Nothing happened. With an unfairylike mutter of 'Bloody useless idiot!' she glared into the wings and waved her wand again, rather more vigorously this time. With a loud Bang! clouds of multicoloured smoke erupted onto the stage, swirling hither and thither as dimly perceived figures scurried about in the background. When the smoke cleared the transformation had taken place. Anna Postl had become an elegant coachman, in black boots, tight white knee-breeches and a dark green jacket with gold piping which came down to her waist, showing off her full figure to perfection. High above her, a coach and pair was stuck on the top of a precipitous cliff. The driver's seat was empty and the passenger was waving his hands out of the window in obvious terror.

— *Take this magic triangle. If you are brave it will bring you safely through all perils!*
Jingling her little triangle, Anna shot up into the air and was deposited on top of the coach.
— *Do not despair, Herr von Reich, I will soon have the coach safely down on level ground again.*

The whole of the back-drop below the top of the cliff was blacked out, then, with Anna trying to play her triangle and hold the reins at the same time, the coach and horses slowly descended to the stage. Anna leapt down with balletic grace, swept off her hat and bowed low to Herr von Reich as he rather unsteadily got out of the carriage. He staggered back in surprise.

— *You are a girl!*
— *There was no one else to come to your aid.* Bashfully *Though just a simple maiden, I could not let your honour perish.*
— *For my sake you made yourself into a man. Now let me make you into my wife!*
The tender embrace was interrupted by Bonafay.
— *Your father! He has his pistol in his hand! Quick!*

The three dashed into the house, which had reappeared, stage left. While they were gone, Florian, the comic servant came on and tried to unharness the horses. He tripped over the steps, had his straw hat eaten, got kicked in the backside and stepped into a pile of dung (which was probably not in the script — what would the censor say?).

Herr von Reich and Anna came out of the house, dressed in their wedding clothes and observed by an emotional Herr Postl and a smugly self-satisfied Bonafay. The chorus tripped on for the finale.

> Florian: *A noble heart, they say,*
>   *Is worth its weight in gold.*
>   *But bills you have to pay*
>   *In cash, if truth be told.*
>
> Chorus: *Ever merry, ever gay,*
>   *We'll dance and sing*
>   *Our life away.*

'What do you think Castelli'll say about it?'

They were in Neuner's Silver Coffee House, hoping to catch the ear of one or other of the established *littérateurs* with a brilliant shaft of wit.

'Damn it with faint praise and a couple of quips about delayed-action magic and speaking names that talk too loud, I should imagine.'

Grabinski looked round, but Castelli was deep in conversation with Bauernfeld and Neuner's pretty daughter enthroned at her cash-desk.

'Well I must say I enjoyed it,' said Kyselak. 'Patsch as Florian was very funny. We all need a good laugh sometimes, especially nowadays.'

'If you're fat and clumsy like Patsch you'll make people laugh even if you've no acting talent whatsoever. He's not a patch on Wenzel Scholz, if you'll excuse the pun.'

'Who was watching Patsch?' asked Euler. 'Did you see Henriette Gruber? The best-filled breeches I've ever seen!'

'She does have a certain attraction,' said Kyselak, 'but rather vulgar. I much prefer Therese Krones. As 'Youth' in *The Millionaire Peasant*. So elegant, all silver cloth and pink roses, and so moving!' He sang softly:

Come brother mine, now is the time,
Say goodbye and do not pine.
Brightly though may shine the sun,
Still it sets when day is done.
Come brother mine, come brother mine
Part and do not pine.

'Yes, very moving if you're of a melancholy bent anyway. And she's graceful, I'll give you that. But she hasn't got enough flesh on her. When she gets into those breeches she looks almost like a boy. Give me *la Gruber* any day. I like something to get hold of on a woman.'

'They say she has a liaison with Gentz,' whispered Grabinski, 'so the chances of your getting hold of her are pretty small. Unless your rich uncle dies and leaves you his breweries.'

'What I don't understand,' said Treumann, suddenly waking out of his reverie, 'is how they managed to get it past the censor. The programme may describe Herr von Reich as 'a rich landowner', but the similarity to Archduke Johann and the girl he's got mixed up with — she is a postmaster's daughter, isn't she? — is so obvious. It may be an invention of some journalist, but everyone knows the story of how this girl is supposed to have driven the coach for the Archduke because none of the usual coachmen were there, and he proposes to her on the spot the moment he realises she's a girl. And her name! 'Anna Postl'! As if anyone could miss the reference to Anna *Plochl*, the *post*master's daughter. I wonder if the Emperor will ever let them get married?'

'What *I* wonder,' said Euler, 'is how she addresses him in those intimate moments. Does she moan and groan, "Oh, Your Imperial Highness!"?' Euler spoke in a falsetto voice, putting an obscene emphasis on 'Highness'.

'But it's not like that at all. I heard how things really are from a colleague whose uncle is in charge of some of the Archduke's apple orchards in Styria,' said Kyselak earnestly. 'True, he's taken her into his house, and she has charge of the running of the whole household. He did it publicly and told the Emperor what he was going to do. He wouldn't have done that if he intended to make her his mistress. And he was very particular to make arrangements to avoid any undue gossip. His apartments are downstairs, hers, and those of all the female servants, upstairs. I find it very noble and rather moving.'

'Perhaps so,' said Euler, 'but all his nobility doesn't seem to stop His Imperial Highness from seeking consolation elsewhere. In crude terms, I've heard that he puts it about a lot among the female section of his loyal subjects down in Styria.'

'You shouldn't believe every rumour you hear, Euler,' said Kyselak, recalling his encounter with the Archduke, 'but the Archduke is a very attractive personality, I'll grant you that. One suspects there are many women willing, even eager, to console him for his enforced celibacy.'

'Self-enforced sillybacy!' exclaimed Euler. 'If I were a Herr von Reich who could swoop down and save some poor girl's father from financial disaster I know I'd be *enormously* happy to allow her to express her gratitude to me, her saviour. Only last week in Rossau ...'

Euler was back on his favourite theme of his conquests in the districts beyond the glacis. Kyselak let the stream of words wash over him. Euler a young girl's saviour!

It was a role he sometimes imagined himself playing in his daydreams. Especially since the incident he'd come across in Hernals when he was returning from a walk in the Vienna Woods a few weeks ago. There was some kind of commotion coming from the courtyard of a grubby, yellow-washed house. He looked in through the archway. What met his eyes was like a scene from the theatre, a real-life tragedy, not the superficial if amusing comedy they'd just seen in the Leopoldstadt Theatre. The figures were frozen in attitudes expressing the strong feelings that moved them.

A debtor's family were having their goods distrained. Articles of furniture, each with a ticket neatly attached, were scattered round the courtyard, a table with some items of crockery on it, an armchair, a set of fire irons, even a stained mattress rolled up and tied with cord. The door to an apartment was wide open, revealing an almost empty room, apart from one bed at the back with an old woman fast asleep in it.

His head in his hands, the father of the family was slumped in the armchair, which the bailiff in his brass-buttoned uniform and cocked hat was trying to pull away from under him, as a burly porter in shirt-sleeves picked up the mattress. A boy of about ten was standing in a corner, face to the wall, while the mother tried to comfort two toddlers. But it was the girl who caught Kyselak's eye, the girl who was the focal point of the whole scene. Simply dressed in a rust-coloured skirt and bodice under a faded blue apron, and a rust-coloured headscarf, she was pleading with the landlord, or other creditor, who stood there, arms folded, motionless and silent in his blue overcoat and top hat. She didn't weep or cry or beat her breast, but spoke softly, insistently, gesturing towards the children and her father, ending in a simple yet dignified attitude of mute supplication, hands clasped, eyes fixed on the landlord. A younger girl stood beside her, sucking her thumb and clinging onto her sister's apron.

He longed to be able to go in and place himself between the girl and the landlord, to give him the money, take the paper out of the landlord's hand and tear it into little pieces. He would turn and smile at the girl, then hold up his hand to stop her throwing herself at him in gratitude. With a few manly words he would tell her to see to her distraught family. Then he would leave. Oh no, he was not the kind of man to take advantage of a girl's natural feeling of gratitude. Of course, it might happen that they would meet again, run into each other by chance, start talking, discover common interests, the awakening of reciprocal attraction …

Such scenes were and remained a fantasy. Kyselak had no money to thrust into a hard-hearted landlord's hand, nor any prospect of ever having any. He had a poorly-paid, if secure post — as long as he did nothing silly! — with little hope of promotion and even less of a substantial inheritance.

No use thinking about Katharina and what might have been. No use scratching old scabs to open up the emptiness beneath. He stared at his reflection in the coffee-house window. He wasn't such a good catch himself. Not only had he no money, he wasn't particularly handsome and he wasn't tall and well-muscled like Euler. He liked to think of himself as slim and elegant, or at least that he would be if he could afford fashionable clothes.

He glanced over at Castelli: the picture of elegance in his cream trousers pulled tight by the elastic strap under the instep of his gleaming shoes, his jacket puffed out modishly at the shoulders, with a cravat that exactly matched its colour above a spotless white shirt. His clothes looked as if they had come straight from the tailor, not as if they had had to have the marks of greasy fingers and inky pens laboriously and not entirely successfully brushed out before leaving for the theatre. He was leaning on the counter, explaining something to Fräulein Neuner with a graceful gesture of the hand. He looked so confident, so at ease — so smug! No, that was unfair. Castelli had reason to be, if not smug, then at least satisfied with himself. He had achieved something, had made a name as a writer.

Kyselak had even approached him once, when they happened to be the only ones in Neuner's, asking for advice about how to get his tragedy performed or published. Castelli had been kind, though not at all encouraging: 'Herr Kyselak, every schoolboy nowadays has a tragedy in his desk. And my advice is to leave it there. Get some experience of the theatre, even if it's just an unpaid walk-on part. Then write a lively comedy with some original ideas. The theatres are crying out for that kind of thing …'

Kyselak wondered whether, even if, against all the odds, his play were successful, he would ever be the kind of person who tossed a neatly turned compliment to Fräulein Neuner on her new hairstyle as he sauntered across to his regular seat, acknowledging the greetings of the assembled *literati*.

Was he at all attractive to women he wondered? Grabinski's sister had said he had 'soulful eyes' when he had been invited to their New Year party. At least that was what Grabinski claimed he had heard his sister confide to her best friend. Well, she was also married now, to a *Hofrat* considerably older than her.

His mother kept asking him why he didn't find a 'nice girl' and get married as a way of 'setting himself up in life' — as if that's all there was to life, a house and furniture, a wife and children! He was sure she had hoped, perhaps even assumed, he would marry his cousin Katharina: 'After all, she's less than two years older than you, that's nothing nowadays. She's so sweet-natured and an excellent housekeeper, she's done everything for her mother since Wilhelm died, everything. And the vineyard and the property in Krems will come to her, to say nothing of the house in Senftenberg ...'

The card announcing her engagement to a young forester in Count Heberstein's service (a young forester, the handwritten note on the back said, who was being groomed for the position of head forester over all the count's estates) had come as a blow to her. It had been a blow to Kyselak too, even though he expected it. The prospect of loss had been depressing, but the finality of the thing done left an aching emptiness. He had to admit that his mother, after the brief shock of disappointed hopes, had responded nobly to the news, had gone straight to her writing desk and penned an enthusiastic reply — *We were all delighted to hear of Katharina's engagement, especially as her fiancé appears to be a young man with such excellent prospects ... Josef joins me in wishing the couple all happiness ...*

Since that day he had had the distinct impression that the women who came to his mother's fortnightly afternoons arrived with more and more daughters and nieces in tow. His mother must have quietly let it be known he was now 'available'. But oh, these 'nice young girls'! Perhaps they were lively with others of their own age, he never found out, but dragged along in their mother's or aunt's wake and forced to listen to eulogies of their sweet nature, their industry, skill with needle or paintbrush, charming voice or other musical accompaniments, they all of them, the pretty and the plain, shrank to blushing, stammering things that hardly dared lift their eyes from the tips of their own shoes.

Whatever they thought of him — perhaps they were so desperate for a husband they would take him despite everything — he was not in the least attracted to these poor mice dragged round by their mothers, like lambs at the cattle market. (A somewhat mixed metaphor, the kind of thing Pichler had told him to avoid in his book!) His mother was constantly listing their virtues and advantages and he nodded and smiled instead of screaming, as he wanted to, that he couldn't stand any of them and certainly had no intention of lumbering himself with a permanent wet blanket like that:

'Frau Antensteiner's coming next week ... Julia will probably come too, such a *sweet* girl and her uncle's quite senior at Ballhausplatz ... he's single, too, so she might inherit, you never know ... Frau Blunzenbach is sure to be there with Antonie ... Herr Blunzenbach was made *Kommerzienrat* in '18 ... business has slackened off a bit since then, or so I've heard, but still ... I invited Frau Hevesi, she's managed very well since she was widowed. I know Leopoldine has a slight squint, but she's quite the lady, despite the fact that her mother runs a Royal Imperial Tobacco and Lottery Concession, which brings in a nice regular income, I gather ...'

The lottery! Now there was a girl he could imagine sharing his life with. He had seen her only the previous week as she came out of the shop with a lottery ticket in her hand. She was pretty, hair in the same fashionable ringlets as Fräulein Neuner, only less elaborate. With her plain, green-and-brown striped dress and black apron tied at the front with a large bow, she could have been a servant in a 'better' household or the daughter of a 'respectable' but not very well-off family.

She stood looking at the list of last week's numbers. Her expression was thoughtful rather than dreamy, as if she were working out precisely what she would do with the money if she won. What were her plans? Set herself up in a dressmaking *atelier*? Buy her sweetheart out of the army and help him establish a small business, a cobbler's, a cabinetmaker's? Hope that one of the young 'gentlemen' like Euler, who were happy to enjoy her company, would marry her now she had money and thus give her *entrée* into bourgeois society? Whatever it was, there was something about her that suggested she knew her own mind, she would tackle whatever opportunities came her way with energy. *She* was not the kind of girl who would allow her mother to drag her round, singing her praises like a shop assistant recommending a particularly hard-wearing length of material. With a girl like that it would be a life *together*, not a life weighed down with some woman who performed her marital duties from the kitchen to the bedroom because it was the expected price for reaching the haven of marriage.

There he was, daydreaming again. What was *he* doing with his life but waiting for a lottery win? And he didn't even have a ticket. Wait! Yes he did. Now that it had been accepted by the publisher, his book would be his ticket, when it appeared, *if* it appeared. Someone might notice it, someone who felt here was a man worth supporting. Or that here was a man who had a contribution to make, a man who would be a useful member of a wealthy landowner's or entrepreneur's staff. The Archduke had spoken kindly to him, had been interested in what he had to say, even. He could picture himself as the Archduke's private secretary ('Very impressed by your style, Kyselak'). Plenty of time in the country, he would be able to go walking as much as he liked. And a modest apartment in the Archduke's Vienna residence. During his regular visits to the capital with the Archduke he would be a welcome guest at Frau von Pichler's salon. Grillparzer would take him by the arm. 'A genuine talent, Kyselak, a genuine talent. If I might make one little suggestion, though. That speech in act 3 of your tragedy, where Emperor Maximilian is stuck on the Martinswand. Might it not be a good idea to ...?'

Perhaps one day he would receive a letter from the Archduke ... No, the Archduke had the common touch, but there were limits. A letter with his arms on the envelope, but from his steward saying how impressed His Imperial Highness had been with *Sketches of a Journey on Foot* and inviting Herr Kyselak to come and see the steward to discuss a matter of mutual interest ...

'... so I asked her back to my rooms to "discuss a matter of mutual interest."' Euler's grating laugh woke him from his reverie. Brusquely he stood up and, to his friends' astonishment, scattered a few coins on the table and left.

8. A Published Author

The October wind was blowing the retreat; at its command, the chestnut leaves were gathering under the trees to set off wherever it should send them; the linden was sickening and losing colour; the beech and elm were thinking of changing their dress; only the Lombardy poplar still rose majestically above the decree of autumn and the oak still displayed its manly courage; in full consciousness of its strength, the conifer, with its never-changing cloak of green, proudly awaited its triumph over the rest.

Unwilling to witness nature in the throes of death, I boarded a ship at Passau and set off home, down the Danube, past the sweet hills and valleys of the Wachau, dear to me as the scene, when still hardly more than a youth, of the first, tentative steps that would eventually take me to the highest and wildest parts of my homeland.

FINIS

Josef Kyselak, 3rd November, 1828

So that was it. The manuscript was revised and written out. He would take it down to Pichler's on the way to the office in the morning. *Habent sua fata ...* What would be the fate of his book? Pichler was pleased with it and would have it set as quickly as possible. He would soon be able to admire it in Gerold's window on Stephansplatz — not, he hoped, stuck behind the serried ranks of Tschuppik's collected sermons!

There was one final decision to make. The title. Pichler, surprisingly, favoured something bold. His suggestion had been, *Austria as it is: Observations on the Current State of the Empire Made by a Wanderer during a Journey on Foot through Austria, Styria, Carinthia, Salzburg and the Tyrol*. No, Kyselak wasn't happy with that. There was something too assertive about *Austria as it is*. The censor might not object, but the police would certainly see it as dangerously political and keep an even closer eye on him than they did on all writers. He still preferred his first idea, the more modest *Sketches of a Journey on Foot ...* It also neatly suggested the presence of illustrations, which might encourage prospective purchasers to give it a closer look, to leaf through it and perhaps even buy a copy. He might as well sleep on it, though. There would be time to write out the title page in the morning.

Then he would join the ranks of the 'authors'. No longer a hopeful with a drawer full of manuscripts, but an author! Even if it was only a travel book he had written, not a work of art, not something that came from within, that was part of him. What difference would it make? Would people see it in his face, in his posture, in the way he spoke. Probably not, he sighed. He would still be the same anonymous clerk whose name, paradoxically, — just his name — was known throughout Austria. But perhaps the Archduke would see the book and remember their conversation a couple of years ago? Should he send him a dedicatory copy? Better discuss that with Pichler in the morning.

9. The Archduke and the Postmaster's Daughter

Summer 1829

'O Heavens! O God! O Jeeesus! Aaaaah!'
....
Kyselak rolled off the comfortably soft if sweaty form of Liesl
and stretched out luxuriantly in the bed, the first real bed he had
lain in for ten days. From outside the window came the mournful
mooing of a cow. It was Sunday and the farm servants were in
the village where later on, after mass, there was dancing which
would probably go on until late in the evening.

'Time to milk them?'

'No, there's a good hour to go yet. Let the beasts wait for once.'

'It's so good to come here after a time in the mountains. Not
just this —' his gesture took in the bed with their two naked
figures on it '— but staying here, being with you. You know, if I
could see myself as a farmer, I'd ask you to marry me here and
now. You know I really mean that, don't you?'

'Yes I do. And I'd say no. I like your visits, but I also like being
my own boss, doing things my own way. Never mind having to
run around all the time checking that my darling husband hasn't
left the gate open for the bull to get out while he notes down a
brilliant inspiration or a vivid metaphor.'

She lay back, her arms behind her head. Kyselak gently ran the back of his hand down her side, from armpit to waist, then drummed his fingers lightly on her ribs. 'I hope I don't cause you any trouble. Gossip and that.'

'No. I don't care anyway. Well, perhaps I do, but not very much. And the country people round here are mostly very understanding. Since Rudolf died ... They all lead the bull to the cow, every year, the stallion to the mare, they know how it is. And you always come straight down from the hills and slip in quietly, when the servants are out, or safely in the *Gesindehaus*. As long as you don't take it into your head to paint KYSELAK, 1829 in large letters on the side of the house! They probably suspect, but let them think what they want. It's much worse in the town. The gossip there was in Aussee when the Archduke kept managing to be seated next to my cousin Anna at meals, or have one dance more with her than with the other girls!'

'Your cousin Anna? You mean Anna Plochl? The postmaster's daughter the Archduke married this February?'

'Did I never tell you about it? No? Well, it was a secret. Was *supposed* to be a secret until she went to be housekeeper for him.'

Kyselak turned onto his side and played with a lock of hair spread across the pillow. 'When did it start? When did you first know about it?'

'It's difficult to say. Looking back there are all kinds of details you see as significant which you didn't notice at the time and would have forgotten if what happened later hadn't made them part of the story.

'They first met thirteen years ago, when Anna was twelve, that I do know. There was a dance for the Archduke and his entourage. During the cotillon she was his last partner and he escorted her back to her seat. She was so excited at that. "Just as if I were a great lady!" she said. But she was more pleased that Ferdl Ritter — he was the handsomest of the local boys — asked her to dance three times.

'After that the Archduke kept coming back to Aussee. But not because of Anna, certainly not at first. He was just happier out in the country and among ordinary folk, rather than at the court in Vienna. He told me that himself once. How the relationship started, I don't know. There must have been "significant" looks, hands gently squeezed, a sudden change of tone when for a few seconds they were out of earshot of others. The usual kind of thing.'

'And people started whispering?' Kyselak stroked her breast. 'The usual kind of thing?'

'Some of the old gossips did. Some women were saying she'd come to a bad end, when secretly they were furious it wasn't their daughter who'd been chosen.

'She first confided in me, oh, when was it? She must have been seventeen, yes, seventeen. They'd exchanged locks of hair, "tokens" of their affection. She was thrilled and yet unsettled. She didn't quite know how to take it, what to expect, so she talked to me about it.

'A local couple had given an impromptu ball, which meant there were fewer people milling around than usual, which gave them the opportunity to talk together for longer without attracting notice. Well, too much notice, there were probably still sharp eyes on them. During a pause in the dancing, people started talking about selecting some of the Jochammerers' music — they're the local band who were playing — to be arranged for piano, and everyone kept playing snatches on any instrument that came to hand. While the others were arguing whether it was possible to set the *Almabtriebsjodler* for piano, the Archduke and Anna slipped out unnoticed, exchanged locks of hair and slipped back into the ballroom again.'

'Did she think he'd marry her then?

'Yes and no. She was convinced he was a decent man who wouldn't try to make her his mistress. And she was right, despite his occasional little episodes with some of the more willing of his female subjects — which Anna probably knew about and accepted. What she hated, was the subterfuges they were compelled to employ. Once she had to take her little sister, who was ill, to the doctor in Neuhaus, and arranged to meet Johann on the road coming back. It was nice to have a long, uninterrupted talk with him, she said, but she felt bad about exploiting her sister's illness. Even when the Emperor finally gave his permission, nothing was settled. She showed me the copy the Archduke sent her. "Clear, to the point and as grudging as can be," was her comment. It said, "I hereby grant you permission to enter into the bonds of matrimony with Anna Plochl, postmaster's daughter of Aussee." No best wishes to his own brother, nothing else except to say that it was granted under "the express condition that neither she nor any children issuing from the union will have any claim to your name, rank or financial provision on the part of the Austrian state or the imperial family."

'It was obvious to both of them that the Emperor was unhappy with the idea, and it was obvious to Anna that the Archduke was unwilling to do anything that would make his brother unhappy. So he took her into his house at Vordernberg as housekeeper, but on the very strict understanding that there was to be no consummation until the Emperor was happy, or less unhappy, with the arrangement.'

Liesl turned towards him. 'Six years they lived like that! He with his quarters downstairs, she with hers upstairs. And he was very punctilious about her reputation, not allowing anything that would add fuel to the inevitable gossip.'

'Yes, I heard about that,' said Kyselak. 'It seemed very noble, but I don't suppose it was an ideal arrangement.'

'Not ideal! It was purgatory! Anna found it very hard. We had a long heart-to-heart talk about it. That was about a year after my Ferdinand died. I said how much I missed having a man about. I assumed she would think I meant not having someone to share the work, for companionship, but I was surprised at the vehemence of her response.' She shivered as Kyselak ran his fingers down the line of her hip and along her thighs. 'It suddenly all burst out. How she longed to touch the Archduke in ways that their situation forbade. How she had stood behind him in his chair one evening and itched to clutch his head to her stomach and then take him upstairs with her.

'Despite her stolid and dependable manner, she's a very passionate woman, is Anna,' Liesl said as she climbed back onto Kyselak, placing his once more stiff penis where it could slip slowly, deliciously inside her. She bent down over him until her nipples brushed the skin of his chest. 'And I gather that she's been making up for lost time. The servants all comment how often they go to bed early, and one even came across them in the cowshed. And not milking the cows, either,' she added as the mooing started again, more insistently this time.

Early next morning Kyselak slipped out and set off along the Grundlsee, heading for Aussee and the Dachstein.

Would he be capable of the loyalty and commitment Anna and the Archduke had shown? Perhaps if it was Katharina he was waiting for? Liesl was a perfect companion, but, much as he loved the countryside, he could not see himself shutting himself away on a lonely farm for the whole of the year. He needed the company, the stimulus of Vienna. On the other hand, he would not want to give up his annual wanderings through the Empire during the summer. To be tied to a wife and children in the city, his only recreation a Sunday excursion with all the other worthy burghers and their families in the Prater or on the domesticated fringes of the Vienna Woods? Perhaps if he had the wealth of the Archduke, or at least a comfortable fortune, he could combine the two, but as it was, for the time being he would remain the Wanderer, with a foot in both worlds but a real home in neither.

10. *Robot*

Late summer 1830

Kyselak took a long draught of his beer. Despite the dinginess of the crowded inn, it was good, good as the beer always was where the Germans had set up their breweries in the Bohemian lands. He drank again. The cool, crisp flavour did much to clear away the sour taste he had had in his mouth ever since entering this town. It had been a mistake to come to Reichenberg. From the map it seemed a good place to come down from the mountains and start his tramp to Prague before finally setting off back for Vienna. And after three weeks gradually working his way westwards from Ostrau through the forests and along the ridges of the Sudeten Mountains, he had felt attracted by the thought of the comforts of civilisation.

Civilisation! The scene that greeted him as he entered the town scarcely corresponded to his idea of civilisation. At first he had been puzzled as to what the huge building was, but when he came closer, the mass of poorly clad people streaming out told him clearly enough that it was a place of work. A place of work for hundreds of people, or so it seemed to him. He sat on a broken-down wall some way off to watch them. The few who came past had no more than a suspicious glance for the stranger as they trudged home, eyes downcast and pulling their rags close round them, despite the relative mildness of the early September evening. Most seemed to be Czech, from the few words he caught. There were children among them, but they showed little of their natural exuberance. Hardly any of them ran around, kicked stones or jostled their friends. There was a dull lethargy about them that depressed the spirit.

After he had completed his sketch of what he later discovered was a cotton mill, the first in the Empire, he set off to look for an inn where he could find a meal and a bed for the night. Around the mill was a maze of passages and alleyways, which he explored in horrified fascination. He had walked through some of the poorer districts of Vienna, but none had quite the same *concentrated* squalor of these shacks and hovels. A larger building served as an inn, but one glance inside told him he would rather leave the town and sleep out in the fields than there. The huts in the mountains might be draughtier and smokier, but they did not give him this feeling of filth attaching itself instantly to his clothes and skin. When he looked inside, the few men drinking there at this time of day stared at him with such hostile expressions he left without even a nod or a greeting.

As he turned into the next street, he was relieved to see that it was slightly wider, hoping that was an indication he was getting out of the mill township. A few women were leaning listlessly against the walls of the buildings, but as he approached, they stirred themselves and fixed him with looks of questioning intensity. Despite the large, flabby bosoms some displayed, they were all gaunt-featured and hollow-eyed. What they were offering was obvious, but all they aroused in Kyselak was a kind of pitying disgust. He did not feel the least desire for these sad wretches. That women, that people should be reduced to this! He could feel their eyes boring into his back, willing him to stop. Although it was early evening and there were only a few women there, it was like running the gauntlet, the skin of his back flayed by those imploring looks. As he hurried to get out of the lane, he was horrified to sense the stirrings of lust within himself. Pictures came into his mind, unbidden, of him taking the last woman he had passed — little more than a girl, she would have been pretty, with delicate features, if she hadn't been so undernourished — pushing her roughly into a dark corner of one of the stinking yards he could see behind some of the hovels, pulling up her skirt and thrusting himself into her, forcing her up against the dripping, slimy wall … Sickened at himself, he wanted to throw some coins to the women, so that for one night at least they and their children could eat without having to sell themselves. But he was too embarrassed. No, too cowardly. All he wanted to do was to get away from this sight, to put it behind him, to erase it from his mind. He stumbled, then almost ran to the corner and out into a small square with a couple of shops and people going about their normal business.

As he took another sip of his beer, a tall, lean man came over with a mug in his hand and gestured inquiringly towards the empty place on the bench on the other side of the table. Kyselak nodded and the man sat down. Almost immediately they were served with bowls of the thick broth that was the evening meal, and hunks of rye bread. As they ate, Kyselak observed the man opposite. He was about his own age, and from his costume he could tell that he was a carpenter, probably a travelling journeyman. He ate slowly and deliberately, as if conscious of the fact that he was refuelling his body. He carefully wiped up the last of the liquid in his bowl with his last piece of bread, then took a long drink from his mug. Before he put it down, he raised it to Kyselak, nodded, said, 'Your very good health,' and took a further sip.

Kyselak responded to the toast and took it as an invitation to talk, if he wanted. 'I see you're a carpenter,' he said. 'Are you travelling?'

'Ah, so you recognise our costume?' the man replied in a north German accent.

'Yes, though —' Kyselak pointed under the table, 'the sawdust on your shoes did help. Josef Kyselak, by the way'

'Kyselak? Not the Kyselak whose name I keep coming across written in all sorts of possible and impossible places?' Kyselak nodded. 'I didn't think you really existed. I assumed you were a kind of myth, that someone wrote it once, for some reason, and it just caught on. Well, you can certainly say you've made a name for yourself. Even the miners in Freiberg, over the mountains from here in Saxony, had heard of you. — Hans Uetersen, by the way.' He bowed slightly. 'I've been travelling this year since the early spring. I spent last winter in Lemberg and I'll spend the next in Prague. A carpenter here in Reichenberg has a month's work for me, then I'll head south. In the summer there's plenty of employment to be found in the small towns and villages, and even on some farms, but once the snow comes building work stops and the farmers have plenty of time on their hands to do their own repairs. Anyway, staying in a big city gives me the opportunity to read and go to the theatre.' He gave Kyselak a quick look, then added, 'And I like to meet other journeymen and discuss … matters with them. Then I can happily spend the summer out in the country. Are you travelling yourself?'

'Yes and no,' said Kyselak. 'Although I like to call myself a carpenter, and learnt some of the skills from a master craftsman in Vienna, that's only a hobby. I work in the Court Chamber, but like you I spend all the summer travelling on foot. In the hills and mountains mostly. This summer I started in the Tatras and have been gradually working my way westwards through the Sudeten Mountains. Where did your journeyings take you this summer, Herr Uetersen?'

'I also made my way westwards, though nowhere so wild and heroic as the mountains,' he said with a smile. 'I meandered up through Silesia and wandered round Upper Saxony, on the edges of the Erzgebirge. I spent three weeks in Freiberg. I might have still been there if the master's wife hadn't decided their daughter was taking too close an interest in me.'

'Freiberg? The mining town? Silver mines?'

'Yes.'

'I stayed for a couple of days in a mining town on my way to the Tatras. Kremnitz. They mine gold and silver there. It was fascinating. They showed me a model of a mine with all the shafts and tunnels, a regular labyrinth. I thought it was very cunning the way they collect all the water in reservoirs to turn the wheels that operate the machinery to bring up the ore, then use the power of the water to drive pumps to send the water back up to the top again!

'And everything about mining seems so steeped in tradition! The clothes they wear look just the same as in pictures of miners two hundred years ago. The black smocks and hoods look like short monks' habits. When I saw them in the early morning, hurrying through the dark with their lanterns, to the prayers before their shift, I almost felt I was observing a kind of monastic order. I'm sure the work underground is hard and dangerous, but it seemed almost a privilege to be part of it.' He took a sip of beer to wet his throat, running through his memories of the town that had made such an impression on him.

'They were a true community. They have a language of their own, with all the words for the different shafts and seams, qualities of ore, conditions in the mine, tools and equipment. They have their own songs — I heard them sing them — and a mine of folk tales.' Kyselak was so carried away with his own enthusiasm he didn't even notice the unintentional pun. 'There was one I particularly liked about a young miner who had a beautiful tenor voice. His singing could often be heard echoing through the tunnels and galleries, and all the miners found their work was easier when they could hear him singing. One day he noticed a little bearded man standing beside him listening. He stopped singing to ask who he was and the little man, who was a kobold, a sprite who lived in the mine, said, "Keep on singing, and I'll do your work. The only condition is that you do not tell anyone." The man agreed and sang while his little companion dug out the ore. He used his magic so that the other miners thought they were seeing their comrade.

'The kobold could dig more quickly than any miner, so at the end of the week the singer received much higher wages than his companions. This continued for many weeks, and the singing miner lived a life of plenty. The others grew jealous and could not believe there was not some magic at work. Eventually they made the miner drunk and he revealed his secret.

'As soon as he had done so, he felt completely sober and was filled with dread. He was sure his end was near and went to the church to receive the sacrament. The next day the kobold rebuked him angrily for betraying him, then grabbed him and hurled him into one of the waggons that brought the ore to the surface, where his companions who had tricked him were standing. "See what you have done!" thundered the kobold, and flung the unfortunate miner out in front of the waggon, which immediately crushed him.

'They buried his broken body with all the rites and honours of the miners' guild, but every one of those whose ruse had brought about his misfortune died a violent death. The kobold was never seen again.'

Kyselak stopped, somewhat surprised at himself. Then he noticed that their beer mugs were empty and called for them to be refilled.

Uetersen smiled and said, 'You're not a writer, are you?'

'I'm only a poor clerk,' Kyselak replied, 'but I have published one book and I'd like to write more. It was about a journey I made on foot through the Austrian alps.'

'I thought so,' said the other. 'I've met a few on my travels. They're always asking for information and noting it down. Especially old customs and stories. Though you're the first I've met who goes everywhere on foot. Most of them like to collect their romantic material in the comfort of a coach. And they usually complain about how slow it is!

'There was one rather amusing incident, I remember. A scholar who was trying to collect interesting folk sayings and proverbs found that the people stopped talking the moment he brought out his notebook. So he taught himself to write blind and kept his notebook and pencil out of sight, in his trousers pocket. He collected quite a lot of material that way, but one thing he didn't collect was the locals' name for him: the pocket-billiards player!

'You can use the story if you like, though I don't suppose anyone would print it. Too coarse for fine Viennese ears, eh? Many's the glass of beer I've been offered for tales of a wandering journeyman, and I've never refused yet. *Prosit.*'

'*Prosit.* I'm sorry I went on like that. I don't know what got into me. In my book I try to describe the countryside as it really is, not some romantic image of it. There may be the odd picturesque sight or custom, but mostly I talk about what there is to see, the people I met and the way they live.'

'Well, I haven't been to Kremnitz, but if you go to Freiberg and see the way people live there, I think your book will be less romantic and, like the miner in the story, more sober. Their work is laborious and dangerous and wearisome in the mine, away from the light of day. Some live in the miners' quarter of the town, but many have huts or shacks among the piles of debris from the ore-works. The silver they extract from it may be beautiful, but what is left behind is ugly. And down in Styria there's a mountain, the Erzberg, that is said to be made completely of ore. Archduke Johann wants to develop it to increase the prosperity of his people. I'm sure he doesn't realise what it will do to his beloved nature. I can see the time when the whole mountain will be nothing but dust and dirt with hundreds of workers, like ants, picking away at the ground.

'Over a thousand people are employed in mining and extracting the ore in Freiberg, and many of them are young boys who spend all day breaking up the rock. And though they don't starve, they live in penury. An experienced miner, who by the strength of his arm tears precious metals from the bowels of the earth, earns less than half a crown a day, barely enough to keep him and his family, even if it is more than the weavers earn. Rye

112

bread and potatoes form their staple diet and they drink a chicory brew they dignify with the name of coffee.'

The rosy glow in which Kyselak had seen the miners of Kremnitz dissipated. 'Tell me,' he asked Uetersen, 'have you been inside that huge building on the other side of town?'

'Ah, the cotton mill? Yes, I went with my master last week to carry out some repairs.'

'What do they do in there? I saw the workers coming out, and they looked like ghosts. I've seen other workers who don't look as healthy as I think everyone should have the right to be. The men who go down the salt mines at Hallein, for example. They spend so much of their time underground, they're very pale, which gives them a somewhat woebegone look. But I have never seen so many who seemed to be so utterly wretched as the men and women — and children! — coming out of that mill.'

'It's the new weaving machines from England. I read about them in a newspaper in the reading-room in Lemberg. They can do the work of ten or, I don't know, maybe a hundred weavers working on their own looms. This is the future. Soon all goods will be produced in factories like that. It will make our products much cheaper, they say, so they can be sold all over the world. We must keep up with the new developments if we want our industry to flourish.'

'But the people who work there, they didn't seem to be flourishing. Especially the poor children.'

Uetersen leant forward slightly and lowered his voice. 'Inside it was how I think religious people imagine purgatory. The constant noise of the machines made my head spin. There must have been a hundred people in the shed, men, women and children. — The owner likes to employ women and children,

113

they're cheaper, they're nimbler and they're more docile. — They were always on the move, trying to keep up with the speed of the machines. The oily smell was sickening, the atmosphere was thick and damp, almost greasy, and filled with tiny fibres coming from the machines as they worked the thread. Many of the workers were coughing all the time. When I'd finished my stint there I found some patches of my skin were irritated and itchy. I hate to think what it would be like if I worked there all day, every day, a slave to the machines, almost a machine myself.'

'I don't want to see it,' said Kyselak, 'even for my book. I have seen poor districts in Vienna. It made me feel sad, but not so utterly sick at heart as the sight of those workers did.' He remembered the pale ghosts of women offering themselves for sale. 'In Vienna it still seemed ... individual. I could still see poverty as the result of some misfortune or of fecklessness or extravagance, drunkenness, something like that. But here they're ... .'

Uetersen completed the sentence for him. 'Like puppets, imprisoned in a system from the cradle to the grave. You're right about the miners. Even if they're poor, they still have the support of a community, a sense of their own worth. And me. I'm not rich, I can't even hope to save enough to set up my own carpenter's shop, unless I'm lucky enough to marry a master craftsman's daughter — or widow, more likely. But everywhere I go I know that even if there's no work for me, I can be sure of a meal, a roof over my head and a few coins to see me to the next workshop. How long it will last, though, I don't know.

'I met another writer, in Zittau, just across the border in Saxony. He was one who asked different questions, questions like the one you've just asked. He wasn't actually a writer yet, just a student, but he said when he did become a writer, one book he would write would be a description of this white slavery, as he called it, and a denunciation of the factory owners. Of course, you'll never be allowed to read it in Austria, if it ever comes out.'

He took a deep pull at his beer. 'As I said before, it's the future. They're already calling Reichenberg Bohemia's Manchester, and where England leads we have to follow, willy-nilly. I come from Hamburg, and one of my friends there went to England. He told me of his first view of the cotton towns near Manchester. He came over the hills — they call them moors — and looked down on a huge bowl filled with smoke from what looked like a thousand chimneys — even the mines will soon have steam engines instead of the old water-driven machinery. At first, he said, it was exhilarating, a demonstration of the power of man to control nature. But it was different when he went down into the grimy, smoky town and saw the thousands of pale, ragged inhabitants.

'They have no age-old, picturesque costumes, no folk tales and no songs. But they will have their own songs, and soon, even if someone else has to write them. And they won't be like the miners' songs — 'See the jolly miner with his lantern and his pick' — they'll be harsh and bitter, they'll be songs about weaving the shroud of a world that has condemned them to a life of misery.'

The next morning Kyselak set off under a grey sky. He had decided to head back for the mountains. A few days in the Erzgebirge would clear the grime of Reichenberg off his skin and out of his body, he hoped. He and his colleagues in the ministry often described their own employment as 'drudgery' or 'slavery', but that was merely jesting compared with what he had seen and heard in this town. It made him angry, but he was powerless to do anything about it. All he wanted to do was to forget it.

On his way out of Reichenberg he walked past the factory again. It was throbbing with the unceasing sound of the machines. There would be room for KYSELAK, 1830 between the long lines of windows, but somehow he wasn't tempted. Near the end, however, he saw that something had been scratched on the wall. It was a crude drawing of a small figure crouched between a large man brandishing a whip and what looked at first sight like a crocodile with a mouth full of sharp teeth but which was probably an attempt to draw a machine. Kyselak contemplated it for a while, then, checking that the street was still deserted, picked up a lump of cement and wrote underneath it the Czech word for slave labour:

ROBOT.

11. An Audience with the Emperor

November 1830

'But you're a writer, a published author even,' said Grabinski, 'you shouldn't be surprised they're suspicious of you.'

'*Sketches of a Journey on Foot through Austria, Styria, Carinthia, Salzburg, Berchtesgaden, the Tyrol and Bavaria to Vienna, including Romantic and Picturesque Descriptions of Several Ancient Castles and their Legends, Mountain Ranges and Glaciers on this Journey Undertaken in the year 1825,*' said Treumann letting the long title roll off his tongue, 'in two volumes, published in Vienna, by Anton Pichler, in the year of our Lord, 1829.'

'But that's not political, there's nothing about liberty or freedom of speech in it —'

Kyselak was interrupted by furious shushings from his friends, who peered over their shoulders at the fat man opposite, apparently slumped in his chair in a drunken stupor.

'What have I done now? I know the Slug reports everything we say to Sedlnitzky, but I've just said there was *nothing* about freedom of speech in my book. It's not like those books by people like —' at the even louder shushing that immediately ensued, he lowered his voice '— Heine or Börne. It really is a travel book, it's meant for people who want to get out into the countryside, into nature. It's to encourage people to go and see what sublime scenery we have in our country. Really, it's a hymn of praise to Austria, not a political statement at all.'

'How can you be so naive?' said Euler scornfully. 'Don't you realise *anything's* political once it's publicly expressed? They don't even like enthusiastic monarchists, never mind someone who might be suspected of strong patriotic feeling, especially if they're likely to *do* something about it. Look at the way they let Hofer be executed by the French. The first duty of the citizen, as the saying goes, is not to come to the attention of the authorities. Not in any way at all.'

'At least you don't try to be witty, Kyselak,' Grabinski said. 'I suppose that's one point in your favour. You heard about that Hungarian chappie, what's his name? Some kind of stone. Agate? Garnet?'

'The authorities would probably like to call him Carbuncle.' replied Euler. 'I'd go for Sardonyx myself, but actually it's Saphir.'

'Oh yes, Saphir. Well, when he published his first witty articles he was immediately summoned before the magistrates, who informed him that wit was against the regulations. He was officially forbidden to be witty or, as the order put it, "The aforementioned Saphir is to refrain from wit in his writings".'

'A Hungarian and a Jew into the bargain,' exclaimed Euler, 'it's not surprising the police keep a close eye on him!'

'And your hymn of praise to Austria won't necessarily get you very far either,' Grabinski pointed out. 'Have you forgotten what happened to Herr Grillparzer's play, the one about King Ottokar and Rudolf of Habsburg? Anything more flattering to the ruling house you can't imagine, and it has a speech in praise of Austria to match John of Gaunt's "star set in a silver sea" in Shakespeare. "This land is fair,/ A fitting charge for such a worthy prince/ … A garland, everywhere in vig'rous bloom,/ Tied with the silver ribbon of the Danube." It ought to have been declared Austria's national play immediately, to be performed on all high days and holidays, yet it disappeared in the censor's office for two years and was only retrieved by chance.'

'And you're writing a tragedy too. Very noble, but very dangerous. Much more dangerous than a travel book,' Treumann pointed out.

'Did you hear the sequel to the Grillparzer story?' Euler added. 'It was whispered round the office. Apparently he got on the coach to Vienna and found himself sitting next to a senior official from the Censor's Office. They'd met in Venice where the man was on the police staff and had been very helpful. Well, as everyone does these days, this *Hofrat* asked Grillparzer why he was writing so little and Grillparzer said that as a civil servant in the Censor's Office he should know the answer to that better than anyone. The man replied, "That's just the way you writers are. You think we censors are always conspiring against you. When your *Ottokar* got stuck there for two years you assumed it was one of your enemies who was stopping it being performed. Do you know who was withholding the play? It was me and, God knows, I'm not your enemy." So Grillparzer asks him what it was about the play he thought was dangerous. "Nothing at all!" the man replies. "But then I thought to myself, you never know." And all that in the most amiable tone imaginable!'

'Is that why you were hauled off to Sedlnitzky then? For an "amiable" chat?' asked Grabinski.

'What? You were arrested, Kyselak?' exclaimed Treumann.

'Interviewed? By the Count himself? It must be serious. Did they find that poem of yours about Winkelried?' He suddenly dropped his voice and everyone looked round, but the Slug had disappeared, doubtless gone to his drunken slumbers.

'As I said,' interrupted Grabinski, 'published author therefore naturally suspicious.'

'If that Winkelried poem ever came out you'd be in real trouble,' said Euler. 'Straight off to the Spielberg and no messing about. A poem on the Swiss hero who sacrificed himself to bring about the Habsburg defeat at Sempach, and to make matters worse, in the style of a Schiller ballad! You know Schiller's anathema to all the red-pen brigade.'

'No,' said Kyselak, 'they took all the papers that were lying around, but I keep things like that well hidden.'

'I didn't even know you'd been arrested,' said Treumann. 'What happened? Come on, you can tell us now the Slug's gone.'

'Well, you know that a couple of nights ago we had a meeting of our club in the back room at Gschwandtner's?'

'Ah, *The Mighty Pen*. Now there's a name that's an affront to any bureaucrat. Either they think writers are getting above themselves, or that they're being sarcastic about penpushing civil servants.'

'Anyway, we all read something —'

'You didn't give them your Winkelried, I suppose?'

'No, just the vision scene from *The Last Knight*. Now if I could get that published — or performed! It's nice to see my *Sketches* in print, to see my name on the title page. But surprisingly it didn't give me the kind of satisfaction I thought it would. No,' he protested at Euler's sarcastic smile, 'that's not false modesty. Somehow it wasn't the same as seeing *The Last*

Knight on stage would be. That means so much more to me. It's part of me. I feel that to see it in the flesh would be like having a son, in a way ...'

'Ah, the great writer wedded to his muse,' mocked Grabinski. 'So you fed them a piece of your little boy?'

'What? Oh, yes. The part where Emperor Maximilian gets stuck on the Martinswand cliff — I know the place myself, from the road it looks completely smooth, as if someone had simply sawn off a slice of rock, though when you climb up, you find there are ledges you can stand on — and the angel appears to him.'

'Oh yes, in the costume of a Tyrolean peasant! Some angel!'

'With thoughtless step I stalked the chamois' trail,
Along the cliff they call St Martin's Wall,
And now I stand upon this ledge of rock
And am transfixed. I can no more climb up
As find a safe way down the giddy face.
O Jesus, in my plight I bend my knee ...

and so on. No one could object to that.'

'I suppose Maximilian's all right — as long as you don't mention the Swiss!'

'You'd still have a problem with the censor, though it's not enough to have you arrested, I wouldn't have thought. You can't have him say "O Jesus", it has to be "O God",' said Grabinksi.

'O God?'

'Well may you exclaim. For some reason Jesus is not allowed but God is, though only if you're being performed at the Hofburgtheater. If you're writing for the plebs in the theatres in the districts beyond the walls, "O heaven" is the farthest you can go.'

'O Heaven?'

'There was a play I heard about. In it an old bigot threatens the young hero with divine retribution:

Such levity will be chastised
With retribution's iron rod.
Remember this: there lives a God!

Hardly sublime poetry, but it wasn't improved when the censor simply crossed out "God" and inserted "Heaven" in its place. Regulations are more important than rhymes.'

'Shut up, Grabinski, and let Kyselak tell us about his arrest.'

'If that's the way the censors work,' Kyselak went on, 'then it's hardly worth writing anything for the theatre. Well, anyway —'

Grabinski broke in again. 'Oh, some are even more fussy than that. One of them for some reason took objection to the phrase "he kisses her" in the stage directions. Every time it appeared he changed it to "he gives her a kiss". I ask you! In the bloody stage directions!'

'And two lovers are not allowed to exit together in case the audience gets the wrong idea!' added Euler.

'Yes, well, anyway,' said Kyselak, 'to get back to the evening at Gschwandtner's. Later on Sauter appeared with some girls, seamstresses, that kind of thing. Now I'm not averse to "exiting together" with one of them occasionally, but that night I didn't feel like it, so I left early and went back to my room and worked on my play till quite late ...'

And so he had still been fast asleep when three policemen burst into his room at six o'clock in the morning, his landlady hovering anxiously in the background. Without a word of excuse or explanation, they ordered him out of bed and as soon as he had thrown a dressing gown over his nightshirt demanded to see any written material in his possession. They meticulously numbered and noted down each item, including, Kyselak was interested to see, lists of tools, materials and pieces of furniture connected with his hobby of cabinet-making. These fellows were nothing if not thorough! He wished much enjoyment to the official who would spend several days trying to break down the code of 'plane, chisel, hammer, saw, nails'. A list of members of an international plot? Of government ministers and other important personages who were to be assassinated? Sedlnitzky the hammer, Metternich the French polish? It was a pleasing idea, he could have worked it up into a nice satire if it wasn't that anything of that kind was far too dangerous. A good job he had thought of hiding the Winkelried poem among papers from work in a file with 'Imperial Royal Court Chamber' written in an elegant official hand on the front.

Everything was wrapped up in brown paper, the packages tied with black and yellow ribbon and then sealed. The officer in charge sent one of his men to find a porter to carry the impounded documents to the Censorship Office. The other, his waist-length tunic buttoned up tightly over his pigeon chest, positioned himself by the door as if Kyselak were likely to make a desperate dash for freedom in his nightshirt and rather grubby dressing gown. The officer sat down in the chair at Kyselak's desk, gesturing him to the rather wobbly chair against the wall opposite, took out his spectacle case, removed his spectacles and, with great deliberation, put them on, produced a notebook from his pocket and thumbed through several pages, muttering words and phrases to himself. Suddenly he said, 'Ah!' looked up at Kyselak, whose quivering was not solely attributable to the rickety state of the chair, and said, in accusatory tones, 'You are a member of a subversive organisation called *The Mighty Pen*.'

So that was it! They had assumed they were safe meeting at a somewhat disreputable wine tavern such as Gschwandtner's in a district outside the walls, but they must have been observed all the time. 'I wouldn't call it an organisation,' he stuttered, 'just an informal gathering of friends to give each other advice on their literary work. It's certainly not subversive. We just meet for reading and discussion. Only last night,' ("as you very well know," he thought of adding, but decided discretion was the better part of valour) 'I read a speech from my play about Emperor Maximilian, which is a humble expression of my devotion to the ruling house.'

'Every gathering is potentially subversive, especially ones which involve writers and discussion,' replied the official grimly. 'However, my duty is simply to gather the material and establish the facts. A more senior, a *most* senior official will decide what is to be done about them. But first he will want to interrogate you. Please get yourself dressed as quickly as possible.'

'Interrogate me? A senior official? But I haven't eaten yet. You can't want me to go to speak to a *most* senior official on an empty stomach. Can we not call in at the the Blue Owl on the way, that's where I usually take my breakfast?'

'No. A suspect must not have any contact with the public before being taken for interrogation. Valentin here' — he pointed to the third policeman, who had just returned — 'will fetch whatever it is you literary gentlemen eat for breakfast from the place on the corner. Give him the money now.'

Kyselak took a few coins from his purse, including the obligatory tip, and told Valentin to bring his *usual breakfast* of milky coffee and two rolls, then went into the narrow windowless *Kabinett*, the box-room that was the standard bedroom in Viennese lodgings, to wash and dress.

He had to pay for the cab to the Police Department himself, but at least it meant people didn't see him being marched through the streets by three of Sedlnitzky's minions.

There the official handed him over to a clerk who passed him on to a secretary who took him to a more important secretary who led him into a large and ornately furnished room.

'Just sit here, the Count will be with you in a few minutes.'

The Count! Kyselak's stomach did a somersault. He was going to be questioned by the Chief of Police, by Sedlnitzky himself! What on earth could he have done to merit this treatment? He was an unimportant clerk dealing with minor matters of financial administration. He never saw any actual money, so had no opportunity for embezzlement, even if he had had the inclination. The only book he had published was surely innocuous, an account of a journey on foot through the Austrian Alps. Even if by some unfortunate chance he had made a remark to which a member of the aristocracy had taken exception — and such things happened, he knew — it would hardly require the personal intervention of Count Sedlnitzky. As far as he knew he didn't have any enemies who would want to make trouble for him. The cellar?! Had some police informer found his cabinet-making activities in the cellar suspicious? Suggested he might be

125

constructing a bomb down there, or operating a printing press for illegal pamphlets? Well they only had to look and they'd see it contained nothing but honest wood and woodworking tools.

'Ah, good of you to come along for a little chat, Herr Kieselstein.' Kyselak's thoughts were interrupted by a rather wizened, lantern-jawed man who had come in by another door and was approaching with what was obviously meant to be an encouraging smile to put him at his ease. The Count sat down at his desk, waving Kyselak to the seat on the other side.

'Well, Herr Kie …' Sedlnitzky thumbed through a file on the desk in front of him. 'Ah yes, Kyselak, that's the name, of course. You have been causing all sorts of people all sorts of trouble. Exaggerated, I'm sure, storm in a teacup even, perhaps, but what do you have to say for yourself, eh?' The urbane smile on his lips did not reach as far as his eyes.

Kyselak was flabbergasted. Trouble? To all sorts of people? He could hardly think, never mind speak. 'But, Your Excellency … I don't … I haven't … there must be some mistake,' he stuttered. 'I'm sure Hofrat Schwondrak is quite happy with my work at the Court Chamber and will give me a good character. And *The Mighty Pen* … well, that's really just fun, congenial evenings with friends. It does get a bit boisterous at times, but that's only to be expected with young people. I'm sure you were young once, sir.' His ingratiating grin was received with an icy smile and Kyselak quickly changed tack. 'We do read out our little productions to each other, of course. But that's so we can help each other with advice. And one of the most important things is to stop each other writing, quite inadvertently of course, things which might offend public morality' — Kyselak knew that many censors were sharper than little schoolboys at finding a smutty *sous-entendu* in the most innocent remark — 'or cause concern to the authorities. Not that we ever find very much to change. But that may be because we don't have the eye for subversive material, not like the censors who can see —' Under the influence of the encouraging smile and unwavering, steely gaze Kyselak was starting to gabble and he was about to say something which could only make matters worse. He stopped, took a deep breath, changed tack again and, trying to sound sincere yet avoid too sycophantic a tone, said, 'If I might say so, Your Excellency, a few words of advice from a man of your experience in assuring the welfare of the state and its subjects would be of great help to us of the younger generation.'

Sedlnitzky grunted, like a fencer acknowledging a well executed parry by his opponent. 'Ah, Herr Kyselak, if only all young people were as willing to learn as you are. But you will have to make up your own mind about what you can write and what not. We keep getting accused of stifling talent. That Grillparzer fellow told one on my censors to his face he held us responsible for the fact that he had written so little in recent years. We serve His Imperial Majesty to the best of our ability and then get accused of nipping genius in the bud. I wouldn't like people to start saying that I told writers *what* to write as well. However,' he said, making a brief note then gently closing the file on the desk in front of him, 'we have explored that aspect sufficiently. I think we'll be able to discover that this time it was all a mistake.'

The slight but menacing emphasis on 'this time' tempered the relief that flooded through Kyselak, but Sedlnitzky was continuing. 'This was more in the nature of a routine inquiry to assist an ongoing investigation. My function today is as what you might call a messenger boy,' — this accompanied by a self-deprecating smile — 'to prepare the way for one who is greater than I.'

With this blasphemy, which none of his censors would have let pass in a play for public performance, Sedlnitzky rose and ushered Kyselak to the door saying, 'There is another, er, gentleman who would like a word with you. Very popular you are just at the moment.'

Outside, the same secretary was waiting for him. With an urbane gesture he led him down the corridor, but Kyselak hardly noticed him. His head was in turmoil. Yet another interrogation? By someone 'greater' than Sedlnitzky!? If it went on like this he would end up having an audience with the Emperor! And he still didn't know what he had down wrong, what it was all about.

The secretary led him along passages, up and down stairs and across a courtyard before opening a door to show Kyselak into a light, airy room, more drawing-room than office. The white doors picked out in the same apple green as the wallpaper, the comfortable-looking sofa covered in a beige material with a delicate floral pattern, the elegant furniture in light wood and the pictures of Alpine scenes on the walls all spoke of aristocratic domesticity. A tall, slim man with sensitive features and a high forehead, dressed in plain clothes that had an expensive simplicity about them, rose from one of the chairs at the table on which was a coffee pot and two cups. Kyselak stood as if stunned. That was —

'Do come in, Kyselak,' the tall man said affably, proffering his hand. 'Sit down over there. I thought we'd take a cup of coffee together. And, Anton, bring us some of that excellent *Gugelhupf.* I suspect Herr Kyselak's experiences this morning may have left him with quite an appetite.'

Kyselak bowed and stuttered, 'With the greatest of pleasure, Your Imperial High—' but he was interrupted.

'Brandhofer. We have met before and if you remember, Brandhofer's the name.'

'Yes, of course, Your — Herr von Brandhofer, sir.'

'I'm delighted to have this opportunity of seeing you again. I've read your book — very thoughtful of you to let me have a copy — and I'm most impressed, most impressed. Just the kind of thing we need our publishing industry to be producing. Your enthusiastic and, if I may say so, extremely vivid descriptions of the natural beauties of our homeland must arouse the desire to become better acquainted with them in many of your readers. But it is not all rushing torrents and mighty peaks. You show an excellent understanding of underlying structures, both geological and economic, and that is to be commended as well. As I told you when we met before, I am very keen to see the spread of knowledge of our environment as well as the improvement of our agriculture and industry and your book supports me in my efforts. Perhaps there might be a place for you at our museum in Graz. I also much appreciated your descriptions all the people you met, those shepherds and alpine dairymaids and such. Ordinary but interesting and nicely characterised. Compared with the city, that kind of people seem to have a sturdy honesty and natural innocence, don't you think?'

Kyselak blushed slightly at the memory of his experience in the draughty alpine hut. Even the Archduke's colour heightened a little as he cleared his throat, presumably recalling the circumstances of their previous meeting among 'sturdy, innocent folk'. But he was obviously not averse to being reminded of his amorous exploits in the watermill, for he went on, 'And your book's highly amusing in places too, Kyselak. I must admit I laughed when you fell down the mountain and your rifle went off, even though it can't have been very pleasant for you at the time. Your gun does seem to have a habit of going off at the most inconvenient moments. Have you ever actually shot anything with it?'

'Not very much,' Kyselak admitted, relieved at the turn the interview was taking. He sipped his coffee and ate as much of the *Gugelhupf* as he decently could without appearing too greedy. But he was still baffled. They couldn't have gone to all this effort, put on this elaborate masquerade just to allow the Archduke to tell him how much he'd enjoyed *Sketches of a Journey on Foot*. Even if he was going to offer him a job — and a position such as the Archduke seemed to be hinting at would be much more congenial than his present tedious task of copying out columns of figures, and probably better paid too — he would surely have written, summoned him to an interview with one of his household staff? Archduke Johann was well known for his affability — and not just to the more attractive of his female subjects — and for the hard work he put into improving conditions in his province of Styria, but surely he, Josef Kyselak, clerk in the Royal Chamber, was too insignificant to merit this VIP treatment?

While Kyselak was desperately searching for something that would suggest a reason for his being picked out in this way, the Archduke was speaking enthusiastically about his plans for Styria, about his model farm, the Brandhof, even about the sterling work there of his wife, as Anna Plochl had finally become the previous February. Suddenly he stopped, put down the coffee cup he had been waving about in the air as he got more and more excited about his plans, and gave Kyselak an earnest look.

'But all this, pleasant though it is, is not why we're here.'

Kyselak's heart sank again. Now for it.

'I am just a messenger, so to speak.' Another one! 'Herr Kyselak, I think I may say that your name — your name! — is well known throughout the Empire. Soon after we last met I realised I had seen it myself a number of times in places where it drew attention to itself. In fact I think I may say it shouted at me from the mountain top when my wife — my then future wife — and I made an excursion up the Erzberg. It was certainly visible and how you managed to climb the cliff-face to write it there, I do not know. But despite our admiration for your obvious mountaineering skills, my wife and I could not help but see it as a desecration of the natural beauty of which you are such an enthusiastic and able portrayer in your book.' He took a sip of coffee, then looked into his cup, realising it was empty.

'People wonder why you do it. I remember overhearing a great discussion among my staff and some visitors from Bohemia when it turned out that your name was as much in evidence there as here. Some thought you just wanted to show you had been the first to climb that particular cliff. One man assumed you'd been jilted and wanted to make sure the lady in question would see your name wherever she went. The suggestion that appealed to me was that you'd had a bet that you'd make your name known throughout the monarchy within three years, only not by committing some serious crime. If that was the case, you must certainly have won your bet.'

'No, Your ... Herr von Brandhofer, sir, there was no bet, nor a hard-hearted maiden sending me off on a lonely winter journey. It was just that once, after a particularly pleasurable, er, experience, I found paint and a brush in a suitable place and daubed my name in an outburst of high spirits. Since then it's become a habit, I suppose. A bad habit, if you like.'

'Like the pleasurable experience, hm? But I have not arranged to see you in order to pry into your secrets, nor to express the slight aesthetic unease I personally feel at seeing the hand of man emblazoned across a pristine wilderness. Cliffs and caves, peaks and gorges are not the only places where you have left evidence of your presence. You also place your autograph on buildings, public buildings even. You have already been given a quiet warning, I believe. But that only seems to have spurred you on, to turn the matter into a challenge. As you will know, there were angry rumblings after the new bridge across the Danube had been opened earlier this year. You had specifically been told not to deface it. The official opening went off splendidly, no sign of even a 'K'. Then two days later a bargee is lying on his back in his boat as he shoots the bridge, and what does he see? The man's illiterate, dammit, but he still knows what was written there. In huge letters, twice the size of your usual stencil: KYSELAK, 1830.

'And now not even the Emperor's property is safe from your paintbrush and stencil. You must realise you've gone too far scribbling on the Gloriette at Schönbrunn! His Imperial Highness is not amused, not amused at all. Indeed, he is so annoyed he has decided to summon you to the Hofburg to forbid you personally to write your name in any public place whatsoever, ever again.

'However, His Imperial Highness is ... well, His Imperial Highness. My brother sees himself as the father of his people, of all his people including, if you'll forgive me, humble subjects like yourself. As you will know, he sets aside two days a week for open audience when anyone can attend. And when he meets them, in their groups of thirty or so, he is all affability: "And what is it that you do? Oh, that must be very interesting, do tell me about it? Is there something I can help you with? Yes, hand the petition over to my secretary." But, Kyselak,' — the Archduke's voice lost it's headmaster-to-naughty-pupil tone and became warmer — 'you may not believe this, but he's a shy man. Especially since that serious illness he had a few years ago. And sometimes he does behave as if he were more *distrait* than he actually is. What I am saying is that when you see him *in private audience* tomorrow — you must present yourself at the Hofburg at eight o'clock in the morning — he may not be able to put his command as clearly, as emphatically as he would like. In fact,' — here his tone became confidential — 'to be honest, you might not have the slightest idea what he was on about. So we, that is Baron Kutschera, the Court Chamberlain, and I, thought it best if I prepared the way, just so there's no misunderstanding. You do understand? Good.'

The Archduke's severe features softened. 'From now on daubing your name on walls and rocks is likely to get you into trouble, serious trouble. Do you not think you should devote yourself to a task more worthy of your talents? Why not write an account of some other region of the Empire? Transylvania? The Bohemian Forest? The Bukovina? You have a talent for that, you know. Cobbler stick to thy last, what? Or' — a twinkle came into the Archduke's eye — 'carpenter stick to thy lathe.'

So even that was not a secret! 'But how did you know, sir?'

'Don't you realise, Kyselak, these people know everything!' Archduke Johann almost spat the words out as he jerked his head towards the door. 'Metternich and his ape! Even *my* mail is read. If I want to send a private message I have to get one of my servants to take it personally. Only last week Prince Metternich amused his friends in his salon by regaling them with extracts from the letters home of an unfortunate English family. A very wealthy but naive and, I must say, somewhat vulgar English family, but nevertheless. Now they're the laughing stock of *le tout Vienne* — and of the English visitors who have *entrée* to that society. There's nothing one can do about it but be as careful as possible.'

Perhaps thinking he had gone too far, the Archduke stood up abruptly. 'I think that concludes our business, Herr Kyselak, but may I just say once again how much I have enjoyed talking to you. If you turn left down the passage you'll find a door into a courtyard which leads into Regierungsgasse. Let yourself out will you, there's a good chap. I hope we see each other again before long. Goodbye.'

The equerry ushered Kyselak into the Court Chamberlain's office. Baron Kutschera surveyed him silently.

'This the fellow?' he asked the equerry. The equerry nodded.

'He know why he's here?' The equerry nodded again.

'Take him along, then, Lautensack,' he said. 'Ten minutes, that's all. And wait outside the door.'

Without acknowledging Kyselak, he turned back to his desk. The equerry led him through an anteroom, knocked gently on a door, waited five seconds and then opened it.

The figure standing by the window at the far end looked like a dilapidated version of his younger brother. The same high forehead and slim features that gave Archduke Johann an elegant nobility had, in the Emperor, withered to a crabbed old age. The Archduke at fifty was still a youthful figure, the Emperor at sixty already looked senile.

Yet the look must be deceptive, at least in part. As everyone knew, he rose early each morning to be at his desk, and two days a week he gave public audience from seven until half past one. That would require a certain amount of stamina, if nothing else, even if he restricted himself to asking his stereotype questions. As always on these occasions he was wearing a plain officer's uniform with no adornment at all, not even a single decoration. Simplicity, mused Kyselak as he bowed and murmured, 'Your Imperial Highness,' was a characteristic of the Habsburgs, at least in this generation. The Emperor Maximilian he was writing his tragedy about had been the exact opposite.

Archduke Johann had also pioneered the wearing of simple dress, the plain grey coat that had become known as the 'Archduke-Johann-costume'. Known and, for some reason, feared. Metternich had had the wearing of it forbidden in Vienna. And yet one would have thought the Emperor, with his taste for simplicity, would have approved. Kyselak and his friends had often wondered how far the repressive system under which they all suffered was controlled by the Emperor and how far it had him in its grip as well. One writer had told him how he had presented the Emperor with a copy of his book, hoping that with a recommendation from him it would sail through the censorship process. Franz was said to have accepted the book with the words, 'I'll read it, but it won't make any difference, you'll see.' There was even a story doing the rounds that he had asked for tickets for the first performance of a comedy because, 'The censors might have second thoughts after the premiere and I won't be able to see it.'

People blamed Metternich and Sedlnitzky — 'the dust on Metternich's shoes' in the contemptuous phrase coined by Hammer-Purgstall and delightedly repeated in aristocratic and bourgeois circles alike. But the Emperor, with his simple ways and exemplary domestic life, they saw as one of themselves almost, the plain man writ large, so to speak. And yet, and yet ... Kyselak suspected, though he would never have said so outside the privacy of his own room, that the amiable dodderer was a pose, a mask concealing the iron fist that held the country in a vice-like grip.

'So tell me, Herr Kyselak, what is it you do?'

The standard question jerked Kyselak out of his musings and he looked at the slightly stooped old man with the watery eyes who was smiling on him benignly.

'The Court Chamber, Imperial Majesty, I'm a clerk in Hofrat Schwondrak's section of the Court Chamber.'

'Ah finance, all those figures. Bit above my head, I'm afraid. But a responsible position, hm? Schwondrak'll keep you at it, I imagine. Interesting work, eh?'

'Hofrat Schwondrak is a most considerate superior, Your Highness, I look on him almost as a father-figure' — no harm in putting in a good word for your boss, you never knew, it might get back to him — 'and the work is ... congenial. At least I can say that my life adds up to something.'

Kyselak's weak attempt at a joke was acknowledged by a faint pursing of the lips. The Emperor did not say anything, but nodded, as if encouraging him to go on.

'And I have many valuable colleagues with whom it is a privilege and a pleasure to work. We are like a happy family, one big happy family.' Kyselak didn't know how long he could continue in this fatuous vein. The Emperor still said nothing, but continued to nod. Perhaps it wasn't a nod of encouragement at all, perhaps it was just an indication of decrepitude. If Kyselak was going to have to make all the conversational running, he might as well talk about things that were important to him and be damned!

'But I do like to get away from it all. I have made many trips on my own, journeys on foot through most parts of Your Imperial Highness's dominions. Especially the wilder, less inhabited parts. The Alps, for example. I even wrote a book about my experiences, though Your Majesty will not have read it.'

'A book?' The apparition spoke! 'Ah, yes. The Empress has read it. Her Imperial Highness was good enough to read out a passage to me. Where you were accused of being a spy in Zell am Ziller. So you showed them your passport. They couldn't read it but were very impressed by "all those damn' stamps and seals". Hmm. "Damn' stamps and seals"! Yes. Very good that, what?'

'Your Imperial Majesty is too kind. I am hoping to write another book soon. About another part of the Empire. Perhaps —'

He was interrupted by a soft cough. The equerry had appeared at the door. His ten minutes must be up. A good job the Archduke had told him what all this was about!

The Emperor had turned away to look out of the window, so he bowed and started to back away.

'Kyselak, ah —' the Emperor had turned towards him again. The watery eyes had lost their slightly bemused look, there was a surprisingly steely glint in them. 'Yes, that would be a good idea. I would be delighted to see your name again — on the title page of a book. *Aere perennius,* what? Certainly more lasting than paint on stone.'

With that he walked back to his desk and Kyselak followed the silent equerry to where a side door led into one of the many Hofburg courtyards.

12. Carnival Nightmares

February 1831

Josef K. inched his way up the rock face. It was as smooth as polished granite. The footholds and handholds were sharply incised, strangely vertical or horizontal grooves with occasional smooth curves where his grip was in danger of sliding off.

His face was pressed close against the cliff and he was sharply aware of the weight of the paint-pot and brush hanging from his belt, and of the void below. Yet despite the slipperiness of the surface, he felt secure, as if his bare hands and feet were adhering to the stone. 'Like a fly,' he thought to himself.

The only discomfort was his nightshirt. It kept rucking up to his waist, revealing his nakedness and wrapping itself tighter round him. He knew he was exposed, but he also knew the slightest tug would send him hurtling down the precipice.

Cautiously he dipped the brush into the paint, reached up and started to write his name above his head. 'K'. As he wrote the second letter, the 'K' disappeared, as if rubbed out by an invisible hand.

He tried again: 'K'. Again it was rubbed out before he could write the second letter.

He knew that if he could finish the second letter before the 'K' disappeared he would be able to write his whole name. It would stay there. It would last. He began to write quickly, with feverish, frantic brush-strokes. But always the invisible hand was quicker.

Disheartened, he dropped the brush and found himself falling, slowly, unstoppably down, down into the rectangle of black below.

As the sheet tightened round him and the lid began to close, he saw the shining granite slab rising above. His name was there. Not written in paint. Carved.

Josef Kyselak
Born 1799
Died

He never saw the last date. His eyes were always drawn up towards the angel on the top. The blindfold angel holding out the book with empty pages. And the inscription: 'A vapour that appeareth for a little time and then vanisheth away.'

Then the darkness.

Kyselak put his pen down and stared at the manuscript for a few minutes, then placed it on top of the pile of papers in the box underneath his writing table.

Another addition to his unpublished and unpublishable writings! But he hadn't written this with even a notional readership in mind. He just wanted to try to exorcise his recurring nightmare by putting it down on paper. Perhaps if it existed there, outside his mind, it would stop tormenting him in his sleep.

He sat back, listening to the raucous singing of carnival revellers in the street outside. Euler and his companions were heading for Sperl's ballroom today. He didn't feel like going. Not after last time.

The two of them had gone together to the *Black Sheep* dance hall the previous week. Things were already in full swing when they arrived and Euler immediately swept up one of the women sitting along the walls, disappearing into the swirling throng of waltzers. As he hung around rather irresolutely, Kyselak had been just as imperiously commandeered by a woman in a black dress with a trimming of yellow roses, her bare shoulders and not very opulent décolleté covered in lacy flounces. With a whispered, 'Can you resist the waltz?' she had simply laid her hand on his shoulder and drawn him onto the dance floor.

When they collapsed, panting, onto their chairs, he had hardly time to get his breath back before she sent him to hurry up one of the waiters, who were having difficulty coping with the throng during the carnival season. Carrying two drinks, Kyselak looked back down the hall. The Sheep was not the Apollosaal, it was even several cuts below Sperl's ballroom. It wasn't much more than a huge barn, really, the greasy light from the cheap tallow candles scarcely managing to penetrate the thick drifts of cigar smoke. Everything was bathed in a yellowish penumbra, like some anteroom of Hell. But that was one of its attractions. The dim lighting and unpretentious surroundings gave it a free-and-easy atmosphere that was conducive to the kind of amorous activity Euler and his like preferred.

The dancers appeared out of the gloom and spun past at frenetic speed, hair, coat-tails and dresses flying out behind them. Watching them swirl up and down the vast space, clasping their partner tight, a trance-like expression on their faces, Kyselak recalled a violent diatribe he had read against the waltz craze: 'The Devil's Dance that sends them speeding down the path to Hell in three-four time.' There were even those who maintained the violent exercise was injurious to young girls' physical health.

He stared through the smoke to where his partner was sitting. 'Young girl' she was not, to go by the amount of rouge on her cheeks, and the energetic dances certainly didn't threaten her physical health. She was a strong dancer, had matched him for stamina and had even seemed to be leading him at times. He had to admit that he was attracted to women like that — or perhaps he was just lazy and preferred to let them do the hard work of taking the lead? But he couldn't quite make her out. There was something imperious and at the same time subservient about — what was her name? Toni? Yes, Antonie Manninger. She seemed to command, to domineer, yet made a sympathetic listener.

He managed to cross the dance floor. 'I brought the drinks with me. Otherwise we might be waiting all night.'

'Very sensible of you. Now come and sit down beside me.' She tapped the chair with her fan. 'You must tell me all about yourself. You said something about being a writer, I think.'

Under the rouge she had a square, rather pasty face with thick eyebrows, but her lustrous brown eyes and husky voice radiated warmth, and he soon found himself talking about his plans and hopes, about *Sketches of a Journey on Foot* and about *The Last Knight*, how that was closest to his heart, how he would do almost anything to see it performed, even just to have it read by the Secretary of the Hofburgtheater, to be able to discuss it with someone who knew about writing for the stage.

He paused for breath, flushed with the excitement that always gripped him when he started talking about his literary plans and ambitions.

She let her fan brush idly across his thigh. 'So. A tragedy is it? Hoping to see Schreyvogel's aiming a bit high, I think, but I do have the, er, the ear — so to speak — of one of his assistants at the Burgtheater. Something could be arranged, I'm sure. But let's have another dance. Pamer's a wonderful musician' — she glanced at the figure on the podium leading the little band — 'but he does get progressively drunk and his tempi get wilder and wilder as the evening goes on. I generally prefer to leave before everyone starts reeling and lurching.'

'Twelve o'clock! Put out your fires and shut your doors!' The usual cry of the fireman in his blue tin hat was rather pointless on this carnival evening, when the streets were still full of people. Kyselak's head was whirling like the dance floor as they made their way back to Toni's apartment ('We can walk there. It's not much more than spitting distance.') Was he going to get the chance to show *The Last Knight* to someone who belonged to the Hofburgtheater? Discuss it with him. And then it would be passed on to the Secretary and Schreyvogel would use all his diplomacy to get it read by the aristocratic director, the Grand Chamberlain, Count Czernin, who, once he had been persuaded to look at the play, would see that it would appeal to the nobility who dominated the audience. He would be summoned to a meeting with Schreyvogel and Czernin. 'Fine piece of work, Kyselak, very fine. Just the thing —'

'Here we are!' Toni interrupted his reverie as she put the key into the lock under the brass plate with 'A. Manninger' on it. She ushered him into a comfortable-looking apartment, hastily took off her cloak and hat and threw them onto a chair with his. 'In here,' she whispered, 'we'll be more comfortable.

'Here' was the bedroom, a boudoir even. Kyselak looked round as Toni lit a lamp with a red shade which bathed everything in a rich glow as the wick burned up. The engravings on the wall were depictions of legends from Greek mythology, mostly of Zeus's extra-marital conquests, as far as he could make out in the rosy gloom. It was full of ornaments and knick-knacks. On one shelf was a collection of decorated glasses such as Franz Karl's father made, with pretty flower arrangements and portraits of the Habsburgs painted on them. He saw the Emperor and Archduke Johann before he felt Toni's hot breath on his cheek and her face blocked out the rest of the imperial family. He held her and drew her to him, feeling a thick tongue explore his lips, his teeth, his tongue, the roof of his mouth. They pulled apart, gasping for breath. Toni, her eyes shining, placed her hands on his chest and said, 'Well, we are a passionate one! And I thought you were just coming with me because you thought I might get your play performed. So urgent, too. We must do something about that.' And before Kyselak had fully taken in what she said, she slipped to her knees, pulled down his trousers and took him in her mouth, her strong lips and firm tongue working on him, licking, sucking, pressing, squeezing.

When he had recovered from the shock, Kyselak was prey to contradictory feelings. The waves of lust that engulfed him could not quite conceal an unease, a slight sense of disgust even, that somehow he was being used. He looked down at the bobbing ringlets and heaving bony shoulders. The way Toni had simply taken him reminded him of his cousin Katharina, of his first experience, and he clung to that memory. It seemed somehow innocent compared with this, compared with the way Toni had let her fan stroke along his thigh, the way her voice rose at the end of a phrase to give it a suggestive innuendo, the erotic engravings on the wall.

As she brought him to a climax, he grasped her head, his fingers tangling in her hair. To his horrified surprise it came away and he found himself staring at an almost bald head. The wig tumbled to the floor as Toni looked at him, semen dribbling down her chin. 'Ooh, we are getting violent, aren't we? But then I've been a naughty boy, haven't I? A very naughty boy.'

Toni stood up, stepping out of her — out of *his* dress. Kyselak felt nauseated, but could not take his eyes off the pinkish-grey, slack-fleshed body, almost mesmerised by the thin black line of hair leading down from the chest to the very large and very stiff cock. He felt soiled that this creature simpering at him could rouse him to such lust. Toni's lewd hand, which even now was stroking his own member, even seemed to have defiled the pages of his play, his tragedy.

Suddenly Toni went over to the wall and held out a long malacca cane towards him. The carved ivory handle represented an erect penis, carved in naturalistic detail, even down to a wrinkled scrotum. Toni flung himself down on the bed, and, raising his flabby rump in the air, whined, 'I've been *so* naughty. You must be *furious* with me. I *deserve* punishment. Beat me! Beat me!'

Kyselak was seized with rage and lifted up the cane above his head. Then he froze, shook himself, took hold of the cane by the other end and with the ivory phallus swept the pretty glasses from their shelf. The last thing he saw, as he pulled up his trousers and fled the room, was Archduke Johann gazing up at him from a shattered shard with one sardonic eye.

Yes, 1831 had started badly. The summer could not come soon enough for him. How he wished he could escape now, out into the country, and start gathering material for the new travel book he was planning. It would be a relief, even if the travel book was a substitute, and a poor substitute, for the books he really wanted to write, the books in which he could say what he wanted to say, the books that would be his contribution, however tiny, to humanity, the books that would carry on his name, given that he was unlikely to have any children to do so.

In this mood, even his beloved walking tours looked like nothing more than an escape, a diversion. From what? From the business of living? Whatever that was.

He stood up and paced round the room. He had moved into it after his parents died within a short time of each other a couple of years ago. It was a pleasant room, much more comfortable than the freezing garret he used to imagine as the appropriate place for poetic composition. There was a respectable row of books on the fine set of bookshelves he had made himself, a comfortable armchair next to the stove, with a lamp on the shelf beside it for when he sat reading in the elegant *robe-de-chambre* he had recently bought himself.

Was that all his life added up to? A row of leather-bound books and a gold brocade dressing-gown? Plus one travel book published to a resounding silence. His *name* was known throughout the monarchy, yet it seemed to have nothing to do with him. It had almost taken on a life of its own. He had heard people say they had seen it written in places where he had never been. Tales were circulating about 'Kyselak' which had nothing to do with him. He was beginning to feel like the man in the story who had sold his shadow to the devil.

What did he want from life?

Grabinski had been promoted and transferred to Linz, where he had promptly announced his engagement to the comfortably off — and comfortably proportioned — widow of a senior civil servant.

Treumann, timid little Treumann, had married his childhood sweetheart and taken up a position in her father's firm. Already he was turning into a respectable and slightly pompous paterfamilias with a house-and-garden in Hietzing and charming twin daughters.

Euler was still content to be the roué-about-town. He was scathing about Grabinski allowing himself to be tied up in 'golden chains', though an undertone of jealousy had crept in after they had discovered just how ample both her fortune and her bosom were.

But his most bitter scorn was reserved for poor old Treumann. 'To conform to the current cliché of the family man with his adoring little wife and happy children clambering all over him shows a decided lack of taste. He'll discover soon enough that marriage is nothing more than a mutual life-embitterance society.'

He thought of his other recurrent dream. The one he didn't wake up from bathed in sweat, but drained of all vitality. He was drifting down a long corridor in some ministry, it could even be the Court Chamber, past door after door, all painted a drab, official brown. They were all shut, with a closed quality that seemed to turn him away. Yet he was sure there was one, somewhere, that was there for him, that would open to his touch. But still he drifted on. He couldn't go faster, he couldn't stop. And every door he passed had the same closed look, until he floated up into the light of bleak wakefulness.

To exorcise the nightmare …

He picked up the two pages he had just written and stared at them. Then he opened the door of the stove and put them in, one after the other, watching them burn, char and turn to white ash.

He gazed into the dull red glow. Then he went back to his writing table, pulled out the box from underneath and dragged it over to the stove. Sitting on the rickety chair that he usually kept out of the way, against the wall, he took the top sheet and dropped it onto the burning logs. It buckled, darkened, and the black ink turned white:

The Last Knight
A Tragedy
by
Josef Kyselak

before the page crumbled to a uniformity of grey ash.

Mechanically he took out page after page of what Castelli had called a 'schoolboy' work, dropping them one by one onto the fire. He stared into the opening of the stove, mesmerised by the flickering red, yellow and blue of the flames. Images appeared and were swallowed up. Landscapes were formed and transformed. One sheet of paper with his name, J. Kyselak, 1826, crumpled to a rock-face like the cliff below the summit of the Erzberg. A sheaf of pages thrown in together curled, the numbers aligning — 27 28 29 — into an unlikely lottery ticket. Faces peered, leered, lips twisted in mockery, pain, despair. His cousin Katharina winked at him before her skin greyed and peeled off, like the flesh loosening from a corpse.

When the last page was gone, he got up and put the chair and box back in their usual places. He stood in the middle of the room, irresolute. He felt relieved, but also empty. He could start again. 'A clean sheet' was the phrase that came to mind. But no tragedies or poems. Nothing that came from inside, nothing that was part of himself. A book describing next summer's walking tour in Transylvania. A means to an end, not an end in itself. The Archduke had read his complimentary copy of *Sketches of a Tour on Foot* and had been encouraging, had even hinted it might lead to something concrete; or was that just his all-too-willing interpretation of Johann's politeness?

He grabbed his coat and strode out, heading for the shrill merriment of the carnival and Sperl's dance hall, where Euler would already be eyeing up the assembled women 'who're out for enjoyment and, by God, I mean to make sure they get it!'

13. A Castle in Transylvania

August 1831

'Diary and Notes for my New Book':

....

Kronstadt (Vlach peasants call it Brasov): ancient Saxon town; remarkable situation: narrow valley, towering alps on all sides. Citadel on Castle Hill looming over town, ruined tower of Teutonic Knights nearby; Protestant church ('finest in Transylvania') known as 'Black Church' because stone still blackened from fire during Turkish invasion 1689; manufactury for wooden bottles used by peasants throughout Hungary and Servian provinces, etc, etc.

Followed valley of Alt northwards; at point where river swings west along Fogaras Mountains continued north to Hargita; noticeable how much neater homesteads of Saxon and Szekler farmers than those of Vlach peasants; agriculture more advanced; authorities should declare 'model farms' to raise living standard of all nationalities and allow them to progress in harmony? (like Brandhof — check with Archd. J.)

Reports of cholera in some towns of the principality, Neustadt, Rosenau, Wolkendorf particularly affected. Johann Josef Trausch, senior official organising measures to deal with disease died of it on 14th Aug. Such devotion to duty common among Empire's servants even though financial rewards not great. Fortunate I am well away from centres of population; must start back for Vienna soon, however; Schwondrak will expect me back by beginning of October at very latest)

Amusing incident of the over-amorous donkey (diff. to include in book?)

Remarkable fortified church in village this morning (Zeytten? Zeiden? — check). More castle than church, built of reddish local volcanic rock (trachyte); massive wall enclosing churchyard, sturdy, squat tower, arrow-slit windows. Asked about it in the inn. 'A safe stronghold,' said the innkeeper proudly. K: 'For protection against the Turks? Surely it's not needed any longer now?' Innk. 'Not only the Turks.' K. 'Who else?' Innk. 'The Tartars! They last came less than fifty years ago. In my father's time.' Tradition of military frontier still lives on all round s. edge of lands of Hungarian crown. Surely now that the Turkish threat has vanished, civilisation, enlightenment and progress ('enlightenment and progress' not in book!) will spread through these once troubled lands, bringing prosperity and in its train peace to all the nationalities?

Kyselak closed his notebook and stowed it carefully in his inside pocket. That was the one thing he didn't want to lose on this journey! He lay back in the late August sunshine and looked down at the castle in the valley below. Beyond the surrounding wall was an informal, 'English' park full of bushes and trees picturesquely disposed about the meadow that swept down to the river. Immediately in front of the house, however, was a formal garden, gravel paths and rose beds with an edging of low clipped box all laid out in precise geometrical patterns. And the castle itself! *Château* would be a better word for this tall, opulent building in light-grey stone, its roof-line an elaborate minuet of spires and turrets, lanterns, mansards and cupolas. He could have been looking down on the Loire, were it not for the rocky peaks rising up steeply on all sides. He examined the building through his telescope. It was well-kept, the flowerbeds neat and tidy and the paving free of weeds, but there seemed to be no sign of life at all, no smoke from its many chimneys, no elegant society on the terrace and no bustle at the back where the stable block abutted onto an extensive kitchen garden. It was like some fairy-tale castle sleeping under a spell for a hundred years.

Kyselak made his way down the wooded slope. About half-way down he came to a clearing with a rustic arbour in a grassy dell. Kyselak pictured the ladies of the castle, perhaps dressed as shepherdesses, picnicking here on just such a still and balmy day as this. Some steps led down to meet a mossy path that followed the sweep of the massive wall. After about a hundred yards there was a door. Kyselak looked round and listened, but still there was neither sight nor sound of people. Tentatively he pressed the latch and pushed. It opened smoothly and silently. He followed the path through the tall trees ringing the estate until he came to where the woodland gave way to bushes. Keeping well under cover of an abundant camellia, he sat down and took out his sketch-pad. It would make an interesting picture: the castle, the epitome of elegant civilisation, against the background of wild and rugged mountains. He would have to alter the perspective a little to bring out the contrast nicely. Perhaps it would be best to make separate sketches and put them together when he was home in Vienna again. He sucked his pencil as he wondered whether he could echo the jaggedness of peaks and pinnacles in the abrupt rise and fall of the roof line. 'The brute force of nature tamed by architecture, the most civilising of man's arts.' Or was it 'The magnate's castle as a symbol of his power reflected in the towering peaks above'? Either way he would have to polish it up, but the ideas were worth noting down.

'"Mighty nature putting the puny works of man in their place," is that what the picture's to be called?'

Kyselak almost swallowed his pencil and spat it out onto the ground as he started in surprise. Turning round he saw a stately figure on a powerful bay stallion standing on the pine needles at the edge of the trees.

'I'm terribly sorry, your ... your gr— ... er, ma'am,' he stammered, 'I could see no sign of life, so I thought the house was unoccupied at the moment. I'm on a journey, you see, gathering material for my book and the castle is so ... so unexpected, I felt I had to make a sketch to have with me at home when I'm working on the manuscript. I make notes, as well, of course, but nothing can match a good sketch ... not that I call myself an artist, of course, but ...'

'But you are a writer and art justifies everything, even trespass?'

She spoke in German, in a husky voice with a slight accent. The tone was ironic, amused even, rather than accusatory. Kyselak stopped gabbling and hung his head in an attitude he deemed an appropriate combination of deference and shame. Looking up, he saw what his friend Euler would doubtless have described as a 'fine figure of a woman', in her forties probably, dressed in a splendid dark green riding habit with a tight bodice. Surprisingly red boots peeped out from under the full skirt. Kyselak knew they were a traditional item of Hungarian dress, but had assumed they were restricted to the picturesque folk costumes of the peasant classes.

'So you're writing a book about us? Where are you heading for today?'

'Nowhere specific, ma'am. I just follow my nose, so to speak, hoping it will lead me to places of interest. Josef Kyselak is my name, by the way, I have a position in the Court Chamber in Vienna.'

She gave him a long, almost calculating look. 'Well, Josef Kyselak, your nose has certainly led you to a place of interest. If you were surprised to see a French *château* in the middle of the Hargita mountains, you will find the interior even more interesting. It is beautiful here, with the delights of nature combined with all modern comforts, but there is a certain lack of society. I'm sure you would appreciate a soft bed and a good meal, never mind the opportunity to take a bath?'

Kyselak gasped and started to gabble his grateful thanks, but the lady had already turned to the servant waiting on his horse a few yards behind her. Speaking in slow German, presumably so Kyselak could also understand, she said, 'Jenö, show this gentleman — Herr Kyselak — to the room in the old tower. Make sure he has plenty of hot water and some refreshment, then give him the tour of the castle. I will be back for dinner.' With that she spurred her horse and galloped off across the park, disappearing into the trees below the steep-sided, flat-topped rock that shut off the upper valley.

Jenö leapt down off his horse, picked up Kyselak's rather tattered knapsack and swung effortlessly back up into the saddle. Inviting Kyselak to follow with a wide, elegant gesture, he set off across the park, Kyselak trotting along behind. When they came round the corner into the rear courtyard of the castle, Kyselak saw what must be the 'old tower', a squat structure made of massive blocks of local stone which stood between the stables and the new château. Jenö dismounted and said, in perfectly adequate, if heavily accented German, 'You must excuse if we go in through the kitchen. I must see to the horse, and the Countess said you must eat.' When Kyselak nodded his acquiescence, he shouted, 'Mártuska!' and a portly cook appeared promptly in the doorway. The conversation that followed was in Hungarian. As Jenö led his horse away, the cook smiled at Kyselak and ushered him into a large kitchen so spotlessly clean it had Kyselak surreptitiously trying to wipe his boots on the rag rug inside the door. The cook placed a small jug of wine and a glass, bread, cheese and some slices of poppy-seed cake in front of him. She disappeared and spoke to someone outside, then retired to a chair at the other side of the kitchen, where she took up a piece of needlework that had obviously been interrupted by his arrival.

The wine, though not the Tokay reserved for royal households and an elite few aristocratic families, was pleasantly fruity and refreshing, the cheese not too pungent and the cake rich and filling. As Kyselak leant back with a satisfied sigh, Jenö reappeared. 'You have had sufficient? Good. Then I show you to your room. We go the shortest way. After you have washed and rested I show you the new house.'

A long, low passage led from the kitchen to the old tower Kyselak had seen as they had entered the rear courtyard. A well-trodden spiral stone staircase in one corner took them up to the top floor where Jenö showed Kyselak into a surprisingly well-appointed bedroom. Steam rose invitingly from a huge wooden tub in the corner. There was also a dressing table with basin and ewer, a mirror and an array of brushes and pots with pomades and lotions, all of which, when Kyselak sniffed at them, had a

154

decidedly masculine smell. Did the countess regularly receive male visitors? Cousins or nephews? He realised he didn't know if there was a count, or even children, but somehow he had the feeling there weren't.

His reflections on the facilities provided were interrupted by the sound of Jenö putting his knapsack down. 'If you'll let me have your boots, sir, I'll see they get cleaned.'

The remains of the meal were cleared away — crayfish and *fogás*, both from the local river, and an airy concoction of apples and egg-white called *Boszorkányhab*. The countess had spelt it out for him. It translated, she told him with a little smile as he jotted it down in his notebook, as 'witches' froth'.

There followed a lengthy conversation in Hungarian with Jenö, after which the countess turned to Kyselak. 'We'll take coffee in the Carnival Room,' she said, leading the way through a concealed door. The Carnival Room had definitely not been part of the guided tour to which Jenö had treated Kyselak when he had emerged clean, combed and smelling somewhat of eau de Cologne and Parma violet hair-oil, from his chamber in the old tower. He gave a start of surprise to find himself the centre of attention of a throng of masked figures in colourful dress crowding round the walls and looking down from arcaded galleries.

'*Trompe l'oeil*,' the countess explained. 'My uncle had it done. The painter who designed it was brought from Italy, but there are also some amusing mechanical devices incorporated in it by a very skilled craftsman from Prague. I'll demonstrate some to you later on, if you like. The room has as its theme the carnival in Venice. My uncle was very fond of Venice. In fact he was very fond of travelling altogether. That carpet you're standing on he brought back from Persia. Beautiful, isn't it? Those rich reds and browns. It's supposed to be a magic carpet. When I was a little girl I used to sit on it and wish to be transported to the four corners of the earth, but it never budged. Perhaps I didn't use the right magic word.'

She nodded as Jenö brought in a tray with two small cups and a silver jug with a wooden pouring handle sticking out horizontally.

'He brought back all sorts of things to contribute to the castle he was having built for himself: works of art, objects, ideas — and people, artists and craftsmen. As you will have realised, the tower where you're sleeping is the only part of the old castle left. My uncle used to say he left it because it was so solidly built it would be more trouble to move it, but I think it was because there's an old family legend attached to it. My uncle wouldn't admit to it, but he could be sentimental at times.' She gave him a smile.

'You're sleeping in a haunted room, but I don't suppose that will frighten an enlightened young man like yourself. And don't worry, I know that 'enlightened' is one of the banned words in Vienna, but there's no one here listening at the door to report back to the Count. The story is — I suppose your book will have local tales and legends as well? "I sleep in a haunted room" should make a good chapter heading — the story is that some time in the Dark Ages ... I know that you Viennese think we're still in the Dark Ages here, but anyway, a long time ago the castle was inhabited by a prince-bishop who unjustly condemned a man to death. The reason is forgotten. A feud? A plot to get hold of some land? A daughter of the family who'd lost her head to an unsuitable young man? I'm sure your writer's imagination can come up with something appropriately evil. It was in that room that he signed the death warrant. One year to the day after the young man's execution, the bishop was found, dead, on the flat rock up the valley. People still call it the Bishop's Bier. His right hand was missing. It was never found, but it is said that at certain times it comes back and can be heard scrabbling over the desk, desperately searching for the death warrant to scratch out his signature.'

She laughed. 'However, I'm sure if you do hear any scrabbling during the night it will be the mice. There's plenty of those left over from the old castle.

'As you can imagine, my uncle was very rich. All of the forests and villages you will have seen on your journey from Kronstadt belonged to him. *Well managed* forests I should add. He didn't just chop them down and let the future look after itself, like some of his neighbours. "Plant two for every one you cut down," he used to say. — There's another quote for your book. — His Viennese friends use to call him "fabulously rich", and I suppose he was, by their standards. He never married. Too much time spent travelling and building his castle and laying out the estate, I suppose. No direct heirs, so that's how I came to inherit it.'

'Yes. I admired the combination of formal French garden and romantic English park when I saw it from up on the ridge,' said Kyselak. 'I suppose that arbour in the dell half-way up the hill was his creation too. Truly idyllic.'

'Oh yes, he designed that. He even had the dell dug out, though you would think it a natural feature. Idyllic? Well, yes it was certainly the scene of his own particular type of idyll. There's many a family round here today who owe their farm to their grandmother's or mother's participation in Uncle Gyula's "idylls". He may not have married, but he was very fond of women, especially the local peasant girls. They would picnic together in the dell. Sometimes two or three girls with him at a time. I found out about it when I was about fourteen and used to go and peep from behind one of the trees. It was quite a picture: Uncle Gyula in his embroidered shirt and the girls in their red boots — nothing else, just red boots. Unfortunately they used to disappear into the arbour at the key moment. Uncle Gyula always used to say lying on the grass was bad for his rheumatism. I hope I haven't shocked you,' she added, pouring the coffee.

'Not at all,' mumbled Kyselak. 'Just one big happy family then, really. Oh yes,' he said, taking out his notebook again, 'talking of happy families, there was something I wanted to ask. There must be several different nationalities living on your estates. How do they get on together?'

The countess smiled at him. It was strange. He couldn't say how old she was. At times, especially when she smiled, she was an elegant woman of thirty-five or perhaps forty, at others there was a stony look in her eyes, almost as if she were a statue from some dark and savage time. Perhaps it was just the expression of a blasé aristocrat who found her bourgeois guest with his earnest questions was beginning to bore her?

'They rub along together,' she replied, 'though there is not much intercourse between them outside business. Virtually no intermarriage, and very little intercourse of the more unauthorised kind either, as far as I can see. They each seem to have their own place. For example my house servants are Hungarians, some of them Szeklers, my steward and foresters Saxon, the estate workers Vlachs and my lawyer a Jew. It's typecasting, I know, but everyone seems reasonably happy with it. What will happen in the future, I couldn't say. Some of the wealthier farmers, even the Vlachs and Szeklers, have started sending their sons to study in Hungary and Germany or the Danubian Principalities. It's all right as long as they're happy to be country notaries or teachers at the various national schools, but what will happen if they start getting more ambitious? I hope I'm not around to see it.'

He sipped his coffee. It was thick and strong and syrupy, as he had expected, but it also had a slightly bitter, herby aftertaste.

The countess observed his reaction. 'An old family recipe,' she said. 'It goes back to the Turks, long before there were any coffee houses in Vienna. Do you like it?'

'Yes,' said Kyselak, inhaling deeply the fumes from the cup, 'I do. The flavour was just so unexpected at first.' The coffee was certainly perking him up. He was seeing the *trompe l'oeil* figures with such intensity he expected them to leap out of the wall and join in the conversation.

'The Saxons have a nice legend about how they came to be in Transylvania,' the countess went on. 'You know the old story about the rat-catcher of Hamelin? The burgomaster refused to pay him the agreed sum after he'd rid the town of rats, so he took out his pipe, played a tune and all the children followed him. Out of the town and into Koppelberg Hill, which closed up behind them. Their parents never saw them again because they came out of the mountains in Transylvania, where they founded the Saxon community. The cave where they are said to have emerged is not far from here. If you ask Jenö he will tell you the way there tomorrow. It's certainly worth seeing anyway, though you'll have to be careful. It's full of bats! They won't bite you and suck your blood, but if you disturb them too much they might make a rather smelly mess on your head and clothes! Jenö's getting your other things washed for you so you can set out refreshed in all respects tomorrow. No, no,' she added quickly, 'don't apologise for your wardrobe. I'm sure Archduke Johann would approve of the simplicity of your *tenue*. Though I have to say your coat did look — and smell — as if you'd spent the previous night, or several previous nights, in a byre.'

She laughed, but again there was that fixed, unblinking look in her eyes that Kyselak could not quite fathom. It was appraising almost. And had another lamp been brought in? The room was brighter, somehow, everything glowed and pulsed with a kind of inner radiance. And the countess's laugh was more like a bell tinkling, reverberating. Suddenly there was a low rumbling in his ear, like distant thunder, nearly deafening him and setting off a torrent of silver waves inside his head. No. It was the countess talking to him again. He pulled himself together.

'... and talking of families and nationalities, we are probably more of a pack of mongrels than any of our subjects. We call ourselves Hungarian, and we are, but I have French and Italian, German and Croatian, Polish and Bohemian ancestors. There's even one Scotsman, but we prefer not to talk about him. And of course we're related to the Hungarian royal house. To several Hungarian royal houses, we've had plenty of those down the centuries. "The blood of Bethlen Gábor and Stephen Bathory runs in my veins!" my uncle used to say. But people would shrink away from me if I declared that the blood of Bathory's niece ran in mine. You have heard of Elisabeth Bathory? No, well I imagine she's not a topic for history lessons in schools, though it might make a good story for your book. Reinforce your readers' prejudices about us Hungarians! She believed that bathing in the blood of virgins would preserve her youth and beauty. Six hundred and fifty of them she had slaughtered just so that she could have a rejuvenating wallow in her bathtub.'

The image was so vivid Kyselak could see the noble blood throbbing in the countess's veins, could see her ancestor rising from the bath, the blood dripping down, her firm, youthful breasts emerging pure and white where the glutinous red was wiped off ... He shook his head to try and clear it. He really must pull himself together.

'And now,' the countess was saying, 'I think it's time to show you some of the carnival scenes.'

In his exhilarated state it seemed quite natural she should take his hand and lead him across to where a pretty shepherdess with a sweet Cupid's bow mouth and golden curls was looking straight at him from behind a half mask. The countess touched something on the wall and the figure's arm swung to one side, removing the mask to reveal a pair of sparkling blue eyes. Kyselak was entranced. Now he was close he could see it was obviously a painting with a mechanical arm attached, but the eyes were so bright with life, when he looked into them ... the figure suddenly puckered its lips and gave him an outrageous come-hither wink.

'Most of the ideas for the figures and scenes came from my uncle. His Italian painter and the Bohemian mechanic simply carried them out. He had a rather bizarre imagination, and being stinking rich he could afford to put his fantasies into practice. They say he had the streets covered in salt just so he could take the actress who was his current mistress for a sleigh ride in July. That's a story they tell about a lot of eastern magnates, but I could well believe it of him. You try now,' she said, gently pushing him opposite another female figure. It was wrapped in a cloak of burgundy velvet trimmed with gold braid and a pale face with delicate features peeked out from under the hood. 'Just press that rosebud.'

Kyselak did as he was told. The rosebud opened out, blossomed, then suddenly fell apart, the petals tumbling to the ground, though still attached to the strings, and appearing to wither. The hood on the woman slipped back into a slot in the wall and her face peeled off — no, of course, that was a mask which had come away to reveal an ugly gap-toothed crone leering at him. The cloak parted. Suckling one of the empty, withered breasts was a kind of homunculus, a cross between a slimy toad and the naked, stillborn puppy the neighbour's dog had given birth to when he was nine years old. It seemed to turn and stretch out a hand — a paw? a claw? — towards Kyselak. Involuntarily, he drew back, then felt a gentle pressure on his arm as the countess guided him towards another picture. 'As I said, a rich but rather bizarre imagination. I hope it doesn't give you nightmares. This one might be more to your taste.'

They had stopped in front of a house — a *painting* of a house — with a large, open, *real* window revealing the interior. Inside was a girl, evidently a servant girl in flat slippers and a dress reaching down to mid-calf. A brush and pan indicated she had just interrupted her work. Standing sideways on to the viewer, she was peeping intently through the keyhole of the door into the next room. The countess pulled a handle — it looked for all the world like a bell-pull — at the side of the painted building. A bell did in fact sound and a door at the back of the interior opened silently. A tall soldier in a white officer's tunic entered and shuffled across the room, like a life-size marionette, until he was behind the peeping Tomasina. His arm lifted in a series of twitches and at the same time the back part of the girl's skirt rode up, revealing a plump bottom. Precisely what happened next was concealed from view as the marionette soldier leant against the servant girl, but the suggestion of his rhythmical if jerky movements was clear enough. The servant girl remained motionless, she was obviously just a painted figure. But no! A loose lock of hair hanging down over her forehead was gently swaying in time with the soldier's thrusts.

The clockwork stiffness of the puppet gradually modulated into a regular, rhythmic ebb and flow of colourful sound waves which were slowly invading Kyselak's body, making him throb in a resonance of sweet purple chords. He felt the countess's arm round his waist as she drew him away once more, the soft pressure of her body against his compensating him for the loss of the delicious harmony.

'Just one more,' she whispered, 'then you can let yourself go.'

They stopped in front of a clock tower. The countess wound up a gigantic key and the hands started to move. When they reached twelve o'clock the ponderous whirring noise set chains of shining silver mountain peaks spinning round his head. At the boom of the first stroke he bounced up to the ceiling and off all the walls, like a balloon buffeted by the wind. At least that was what it felt like, but it couldn't be true because the countess was still holding him firmly round the waist.

The front of the tower slid aside and a kind of circular track glided out. As it revolved, figures appeared. ('Just like the clock in Prague,' Kyselak thought. 'Ah, the Bohemian mechanic!') They represented church dignitaries: bishops and priests, abbots and abbesses, monks and nuns. As they passed, their clothes flew off and they performed various sexual acts with each other, an obscene round-dance of fat pink bodies heaving and shaking. When the last stroke sounded, a skeleton appeared, waving its scythe which, as they disappeared back into the tower, it thrust up the arse of the cardinal in front of him.

'A dance of death. Very moral in the end,' said the countess.

Kyselak was lying on the floor. How he got there he had no idea. Drifted down, perhaps? He had certainly not felt any impact of hitting the ground. He felt free, unencumbered, the cool air wafted over his skin.

He was lying down and yet he was floating, floating through the air on something warm and soft. Of course! He was on the Persian carpet, the magic carpet! He felt it undulating beneath him as he surged and plunged over the heads of the carnival figures gathered in the square below. His body curved, responding to every swoop and soar, merging with the carpet that bore him up. He *was* the carpet, and the countess was kneeling on it, thighs splayed, back straight, her iridescent skin a silky ripple of blues and greens. Her hair fluttered round her head like a thousand humming birds, her firm, round breasts were encircled with pulsating coronas of vibrant silver which rang in his ears and from the point where they joined a powerful sweetness ran through him, setting his whole body tingling.

The sensation of lightness and power intensified as he circled the tower, spiralling upwards and upwards until, in a sunburst of resonant colour, he suddenly plummeted down in free fall and skimmed along the ground, like an ash-key on the gusts of a fitful breeze, before coming to rest, drained, inert, an empty seed husk on an infinity of rust-red, shifting sands.

'If you take the path past the rock they call the Bishop's Bier — you know where that is? — and follow it up the valley for a league or so, you will come to the hunter's track. It is well made and they look after it well. It starts just past an oak that was struck by lightning in the storm three years ago, and it goes up to the saddle at an easy gradient. The path continues over and down the other side, then turns left and runs across the face of the hill, below the cliffs to the next saddle. Some of the local young men go along the ridge. It is a scramble down the far side, they say, but there are magnificent views over a huge ocean of forest stretching for miles and miles on every side, the peaks like rocky islands in a sea of green.'

Jenö paused for a moment and frowned, as if such poetic touches were out-of-place in a servant. 'The cave with the bats, the Almasch Cave, is in the hillside on the far side of the saddle. It is easy to see when you are there. You might even come across a bear. They're not really dangerous, as long as you leave them alone, and you have your rifle anyway, if you need it. But are you sure you want to set off now, sir? The weather is not very inviting and the countess said we must make you welcome for as long as you wish to stay.'

'Thank you, but no,' said Kyselak. 'I must get on and I'm used to tramping the country in all weather, as you could probably tell from the state of my clothes. You end up forgetting how wonderful it feels to put on a clean shirt. And all my clothes have been washed and dried and pressed! Even the buckle on my knapsack has been mended. Someone must have stayed up all night.'

'That was Mártuska. She's getting old now and she doesn't sleep very much anyway. She likes having things to do, she says it's too quiet for her now, not like when the old count used to bring all his friends. There's only the countess and her maid,' he explained. 'I live with my family in a house by the dairy farm. And,' he allowed himself a smile, the only one Kyselak had seen on his rather solemn if open features, 'Mártuska says you need looking after. You probably remind her of her grandson. He went away to Pest to study and he lives there now. He only comes back here occasionally.

'If you are determined to leave now, sir, we will go out through the kitchen. The countess said to give you her greetings. She will not be up until much later, but she left orders for a packet of food to be prepared for you and for your flask to be filled. With some of the wine from an estate the family owns north of Arad. It's very refreshing.'

They went along the stone-flagged corridor to the kitchen, where a beaming Mártuska was waiting with a large packet of food. As he took it, Kyselak tried to slip a coin into her hand, but she closed his fingers over it and pushed his hand away, at the same time bursting into a torrent of Hungarian.

'She says it is not necessary,' translated Jenö. 'She says it is a pleasure for her to look after a young gentleman. She says' — Kyselak could have sworn Jenö almost grinned — 'to put it with the money you're saving up for when you get married.'

Mártuska nodded and smiled, and Kyselak said, 'Köszönöm!' As 'Pardon!' seemed to do for 'Sorry', 'Thank you' was the sum total of his Hungarian. He put on his coat, turned up the collar and stepped out into the steady rain.

He had woken up in the morning feeling strangely relaxed, despite a slight throbbing in his head. Every muscle seemed loose and lithe, and he was happy to stretch out luxuriantly and huddle back into the embrace of the warm down quilt. The dull grey light and the patter of raindrops on the window were no encouragement to get out of bed for an early start. Eventually, and by the exertion of considerable will-power, he managed to force himself to get up. His knapsack, brushed clean of mud and the buckle that had been hanging by a loose thread mended, was leaning against the wall. All his clothes were clean and neatly stacked on the table above it. And he was naked, absolutely naked! He had no recollection at all of how he had found his way back to his room last night, and he decided it was best not to enquire, not even to think about it.

The climb up to the ridge had cleared his head. He had not met anyone on the way apart from a solitary mushroom gatherer in the woods who had wished him good day and, he assumed, passed some remark about the inclement weather. The 'ocean of green with the peaks standing out like rocky islands' was nowhere to be seen, the only sea was a sea of mist. But the line of the ridge was easy to follow with some sporting, but not too difficult buttresses to clamber over. Scrambling down to the saddle was the most awkward passage, especially with the wet rock. At one point he had to turn round to descend a vertical face. There were footholds, but that first step out into the air demanded he keep his nerve until he felt the firmness of the protruding rock beneath his foot. 'If I slipped and fell,' he asked himself, 'would anyone find me?' Would he lie there with a broken leg until he died of starvation and exposure? Would his body decompose until some huntsman, or a shepherd looking for a stray sheep found his bleached bones on the ledge below? Would anyone notice his absence? Was there anyone to care? With an exasperated shake of the head he put these thoughts out of his mind and climbed down the slab foothold by foothold. Once he was out on the rock it was straightforward, like going down a ladder, and he enjoyed the alternation of handhold, foothold, handhold, foothold. As he swung down he hummed to himself, then sang softly as he made his way with springy steps down the last grassy slope:

I wander on, weighed down by care,
And sighing, ever asking, Where?
Asking where?

Where are you, where are you, land where joy abounds?
Long sought, long dreamt, but never found.
O land of hope's eternal spring,
Where roses bloom and skylarks sing ...

Across the saddle the cleft leading to the cave was easy to spot. The rain had thinned to a faint drizzle and the mist was starting to lift. He picked his way through the rocks up to the cave, avoiding the profusion of alpine salamanders tempted out by the wet conditions. Country folk in Austria believed they were poisonous, and they certainly looked venomous with their glistening black skin, bulbous eyes and lines of bumps and ridges down their backs. But they were harmless, as Kyselak knew, and he regarded them as friendly companions, often the only other creatures out in weather like this, apart from himself.

The cave was dry. A few bats flew up as he went in, but when he sat down they fluttered around for a minute or two and then returned to their roosts. He could see them, in serried ranks along the roof where the cavern stretched into the blackness, a dark womb in the mountain. He would not disturb them further by lighting a candle or flare. He decided to have a bite to eat from Mártuska's provisions, a mouthful of wine, and wait to see if the mist would clear and the sun come out. The cold chicken he ate with a slice of rye bread was delicious, the skin crisp and encrusted with paprika. As he ate, the smooth wall inside the entrance seemed to beckon to him. It was just the place he would have written his name, before the imperial veto. But who would see it here? As the countess had said, there was no one who was going to report back to Vienna. Anyway, what did it matter? His life was going nowhere. No grand passion, no wife, no family, no immortal works from his pen, just emptiness. Another 'amiable chat' with Sedlnitzky, even a spell in the Spielberg prison wouldn't make much difference.

After his interview with the Emperor he had ceremonially consigned the stencil to the flames of his stove, but he had not bothered to remove the pot of paint and brush from his knapsack. Unless Mártuska had thrown it out when mending the buckle? No, it was still there. One last signature, then, as a farewell to the carefree days on his youth.

Telling himself not to be so sentimental, he carefully wrote his name and the date on the wall. In full this time, JOSEF KYSELAK, 6th SEPTEMBER 1831. — and with a full stop at the end: period. He lay back, replete and comfortable, his limbs aching a little from the exertion the ridge had demanded and suffused with a slight, delicious drowsiness from whatever had happened the previous night.

As he lay there, he pictured the hundreds of Hamelin children coming through the mountain, walking in the pitch darkness without stumbling, mesmerised by the music, stepping with the surefootedness of sleep-walkers. He could almost hear their voices, their shrill cries as they saw the sunlit sky at the end of the cleft, their squeals of delight as they looked out over the green land spread out below.

He woke up and realised he must have been sleeping. Outside, a shaft of sunlight pierced the clouds and lit up the steep face he had started down with such trepidation only an hour or so ago.

It was an easy birth,
she said, no trauma, just
a coming-out into joy.
The music drew us on,
we plunged into its sweet,
long-drawn-out melody,
a vein of sound
through the dark inside of
the mountain, like silver
through the rock. Our feet moved
in time to the notes,
securely, without stumbling.
Sight was not necessary,
but when it came it was
a glorious revelation,
a radiance breaking,
inextinguishable, from the sky,
the cave entrance a
door just for us
to a sunlit land
beyond the forests.

14. Cholera

October 1831

Kyselak made his way unsteadily back home. His head ached, his legs, usually so strong from his summer excursions, were sore and he had spewed in a narrow close between two houses. It must be about four o'clock in the morning. All he wanted to do was to get to his room, lie down on his bed and sleep.

It had been a mistake to stay out so long, it had been a mistake to drink so much. It had been a mistake to agree to go on to Gschwandtner's at all, but Euler's enthusiasm was infectious and life in Vienna was depressing just at the moment.

All around him the sleeping city was silent, but as he stumbled down Pfeilgasse he heard an outburst of raucous singing and the sound of shattering glass from the direction of Lerchenfelderstraße.

Why should an evening which had started so pleasantly have to end in this wretched feeling of pain and nausea? Although October, it was still mild and they had strolled out to one of their habitual wine-taverns in Dornbach, discussing the normal things: actresses, the latest plays and books, their plans for the winter months. After Grabinski's and Treumann's defection Euler had quickly gathered a new group of intimates around him. Their talk had perhaps been so determinedly normal that it was abnormal. There had been something desperate about the way they had avoided the one topic that had dominated conversation in Vienna for the last month, the cholera epidemic.

But it was always present, always at the back of their minds, so that there was a tingle of apprehension beneath even the most innocuous exchange. The evening had gradually become more and more frenetic, so that when Euler had stood up and announced he was going to Gschwandtner's to drink the night away, they had all followed in a jostling, meandering wake. There things were already in full swing. Social barriers seemed to be disintegrating, as well-dressed gentlemen rubbed shoulders with tradesmen, labourers and market porters. Everyone there seemed determined to squeeze one last drop out of life before succumbing to the dreaded plague. They seemed almost relieved to be able to throw off the restraint of a social order in which the family, the respectable middle-class family, was the touchstone of morality for almost everyone, from the carpenter in the Alsergrund to the Emperor in the Hofburg.

Eventually Euler gathered his flock together again and declared he was going to pay the 'ladies' a visit they would not forget for a long time. Again they set off, Euler at their head, singing and shouting. Here Kyselak had parted company with them. Not for any reason about which he could feel morally superior, simply because he felt so awful he was not sure he would be able to make it as far as his room in the Josefstadt. Euler's voice echoed among the buildings, gradually growing fainter:

O my darling Augustine, Augustine, Augustine,
O my darling Augustine,

Everything's dead.
The cow is dead, the horse's dead
The Prince's dead, the Count is dead
O my darling Augustine,
Everything's dead.

He finally reached home, staggered up the stairs, took a large drink from the jug of boiled water his landlady had brought up earlier in the day and collapsed on his bed.

If only he had known what conditions in the city were like, he wouldn't have returned from his summer tramp, but stayed somewhere in the country. Hardly anyone was behaving normally under the pressure of fear of the mysterious disease that had made its slow but apparently inexorable way from Asia to Europe. The authorities had been galvanised into an untypical burst of activity and the strict measures they had taken, including ten days' quarantine for anyone coming from anywhere that sounded remotely as if it might be a source of cholera, had contributed to the air of barely suppressed panic you could almost taste in the streets. You could hardly walk past a house without being assailed by the smell of fumigation or doused in vinegar from a disinfectant spray. Some shopkeepers even insisted on customers disinfecting coins before handing them over in payment.

At the sound of the bell warning that a cholera patient was being transported to hospital, everyone rushed to hide in the nearest house entrance. But most peeped out and shivered in horror at the sight of the bearers in their black taffeta overalls. Kyselak, who determinedly continued to walk round the city as usual, almost challenging the disease to come and put an end to his empty existence, had only seen a dozen or so such processions, so there were probably far fewer cases than people believed.

Initially doctors going to visit cholera patients in their protective armour of oilcloth coats and hoods, their faces completely shielded by a kind of carnival mask with a pointed nose and thick glasses, had been seen as figures of doom, but they were rapidly becoming objects of derision, especially to the sharp-tongued apprentices and delivery boys. Many had already abandoned their patent anti-cholera garb.

Some people stayed at home with a hoard of food and sealed-up doors and windows. Others maintained that fresh air was the thing and kept their windows wide open. Many of those who went out crept along in the shadow of buildings, as if the disease could be outwitted by stealth. Others determinedly went about their business in a withdrawn, self-enclosed manner, as if they were being borne along inside a transparent bubble. Even the few who managed to behave normally had a subconscious air of defiance about them, as if the slightest jolt could topple them over into the manic activity of Euler and his fellow orgiasts.

Kyselak settled into the soft clutches of the eiderdown. His head was still throbbing and his guts felt as if they had been wrenched out of position, but at least the desire to vomit had faded. A good sleep was what he needed.

His back and legs still ached. It was as if he had spent the last few days picking his way across the jumble of a boulder field, striding through knee-high grass and heather, then inching his way down an unstable slope where a glacier had just receded, rocks abruptly coming loose and crashing down beside him.

Everything was hazy, misty. The cloud had accompanied him down into the valley. As he sat on the bench under the lime tree outside the village inn, stretching out his weary legs, the villagers crowded round, pleading with him not to attempt the Großglockner, not in weather like this, not without a guide. An old man warned him against the pass, another peasant adding that it was a place where avalanches often caught the unwary.

But Kyselak pulled himself to his feet, smiled at the girl whose look seemed to be pleading with him to stay, and set off through the mist, the roar of the torrent in his ears. He knew he had to climb, up and up, to the highest summit. Strangely, as he trudged through the snow and ice, his weariness seemed to leave him. The mist around lightened too, he could sense the warmth and the brightness of the sun far overhead, and the snowy slopes began to gleam as if with an inner brilliance. His step was lighter, springier as he ascended the slope up to the main ridge. He put down his knapsack, rifle and heavy coat and continued unencumbered, floating, wing-heeled, towards the summit.

He could see it now, a pinnacle of brightness in the surrounding lucency. As he soared upwards the sun broke through, a shining door, a gate of light to the radiant world beyond, and a voice whispered in his ear, 'No need for your paint and stencil here, Josef, your name is already written.'

An extract from:

Constant von Wurzbach: *Biographical Dictionary of the Empire of Austria, Containing Sketches of the Lives of Noteworthy Persons who Lived in the Imperial State and in its Crownlands between 1750 and 1850.* (60 vols., Vienna, 1856-91.)

> **Kyselak**, Josef: eccentric,
> b. Vienna around the year
> 1799, d. there of cholera
> between 16 and 26 October,
> 1831.